# I'LL BE THERE FOR YOU

## JESSA HALLIWELL

I'll Be There For You: A Dark Stalker Romance

By Jessa Halliwell

Copyright © 2026 by Jessa Halliwell

Cover art and design by Bee at Bitter Sage Designs

Character art by Jessa Halliwell

# CONTENTS

# IBTFY PLAYLIST

**Prologue**
Waiting For Never - Post Malone
**Chapter One**
Everything You Want - Vertical Horizon
**Chapter Two**
Heads Will Roll - The Yeah Yeah Yeahs
**Chapter Three**
Animals - Maroon 5
**Chapter Four**
Breathe Me - Sia
**Chapter Five**
Again - Lenny Kravitz
**Chapter Six**
Uninvited - Alanis Morissette
**Chapter Seven**
We're Going to Be Friends - The White Stripes
**Chapter Eight**
Sugar - Sleep Token
**Chapter Nine**

# PROLOGUE

DAHLIA

*Age 17, Carnesville, Georgia*

NO ONE TELLS YOU WHAT YOU'RE SUPPOSED TO WEAR TO your ex's murder trial.

I spent twenty minutes staring at my closet this morning. Agonizing over the choice before finally settling on a plain black sweater and a pair of dark jeans that I hoped would help keep me invisible. Kind of stupid in hindsight, considering it probably doesn't matter. Everyone in this town recognizes me by now.

The wooden bench creaks beneath me as I take a seat in one of the only open spots left in the courtroom. Dozens of eyes laser their focus on me and, as if on cue, the whispering starts.

I almost didn't show up today.

After testifying last month, I promised myself I'd never set foot in this place again. But the verdict is in, and staying away just wasn't an option.

I think I needed to hear it for myself. Needed to know, beyond a shadow of a doubt, that *he* wouldn't be able to hurt anyone else again.

Christian sits at the defense table like it's just another Tuesday for him. His posture is relaxed, his suit is pressed, and his golden-brown hair is styled perfectly, with not even a strand out of place. He looks normal. Sane even. Nothing like the monster he's proven himself to be.

"That's her." A woman behind me whispers. "The girlfriend."

*Ex-girlfriend,* I mentally correct, *not that it makes a difference to any of these people.*

"I still think she put him up to it." Another woman whispers back. "I know the family. He was a good boy until he met her."

Swallowing hard, I wrap my fingers around the edge of the bench beneath me and let my nails dig into the thick varnish to try to help ground myself.

I didn't put Christian up to anything. *I know I didn't.* But I can't help but feel the truth in what she's saying.

I may not have had any idea what he was planning, but I caused this. I was the catalyst that drove Christian to do what he did that night, and I deserve to carry as much of the blame as he does.

"I don't know how the hell she lives with herself." The first woman adds, letting hate radiate from every syllable.

The truth is I don't.

I breathe, I eat, and I sleep when I can. But I don't live. I just exist. And honestly, after everything that happened, I'm not sure I even deserve that.

"She doesn't care." A man hisses, not even bothering to lower his voice. "They were her parents, for God's sake, but that didn't matter to her."

At the mention of my parents, grief slams into me with such crushing force it nearly knocks the wind out of me. My head drops, and the tears that I've been desperately trying to rein in since I got here finally spill over.

*Fuck.*

*I can't do this. I can't be here.*

*It's too hard. It's too much.*

I shake my head, and my watery gaze drifts to the empty seats beside me. The ones Mom and Dad would be sitting in if it weren't for me. I can almost feel Dad's hand patting my knee, in that awkward, stoic way of his. Can almost hear Mom's lovingly teasing words in my ear.

*Don't cry, Anak. Papangit ka.*

*Don't cry, daughter. You'll get ugly.*

A sad smile spreads across my face.

*God, I miss them.*

And it's not just their presence that I miss most; it's all the little things. Their laughs. The ones that were too loud and way too infectious. Their food. No one, and I mean no one, can cook like my dad. Their love. It was never really expressed out loud, and honestly, I used to resent them for that, but now that I know what it feels like to be without it, I know I felt it in everything they did for me. *Every fucking thing.*

More unwelcome tears slide down my cheeks, and I swipe them away with the sleeve of my sweater and try to pull myself together.

*Stop it. Stop crying right now. You need to be strong, if not for yourself, for them.*

Blowing out a shaky breath, I blink back my tears and force my head up, only to find Christian turned in his seat, staring at me.

I've seen him a handful of times over the course of the thirteen-month trial, but looking him in the eye hasn't gotten any easier. It's like my brain still hasn't fully accepted that the monster sitting on trial in front of me is the same boy I fell in love with freshman year.

"I love you." Christian mouths, the words, silent, yet somehow clear as day.

*And I should have never loved you.* I think to myself, fixing my eyes on the weathered wainscoting behind him.

Christian glares at me, and after a few tense seconds, he sighs and finally turns back around in his seat.

Seconds later, the bailiff clears his throat, and the courtroom dulls to a hushed silence. "All rise." He says. "The Honorable Judge Walker is now entering the courtroom."

Benches groan and metal chair legs screech across the scuffed terrazzo floor. A door near the front of the room opens, and the judge steps in with his black robe billowing behind him. He takes his seat, and the bailiff orders the rest of us to do the same.

The judge places his wiry glasses on the tip of his bulbous nose and looks at the jury. "Members of the jury, have you reached a verdict?"

A bald man in his late forties rises from his seat in the jury box. "We have, Your Honor. On two counts of murder in the first degree, we find the defendant Christian Sanders… **guilty**."

I don't hear the rest of the verdict.

I'm too busy trying to remember how to breathe.

The courtroom erupts in chaos around me, with everything ranging from screams to cheers to full-on sobs echoing through the tiny courtroom. A sharp wail rises above the rest, Christian's mother, and the sound of her agony is so palpable, just hearing it brings fresh tears to my eyes.

I drag my gaze over to Christian, and he doesn't even look fazed. He's still sitting at the defense table with his jaw flexed and an otherwise blank expression on his face. Two officers approach him with cuffs in hand, and as his stone-faced lawyers rise from their seats, Christian turns around to face the courtroom.

"I did this for us, Dollface!" He yells, looking directly at me. His voice is laced with so much conviction it makes my whole body lock up. "I fucking love you. I always have, and I always will."

A murmur ripples through the crowd as accusing glances dart my way. If people didn't notice I was here before, they do now.

People shout over one another as reporters scramble toward me, and cameras flash like strobe lights from every direction.

I need to get the hell out of here. I need to leave right now before it gets worse. But the exit feels miles away, and the thought of turning around to face the crowd is nauseating.

A hand touches my shoulder, and I flinch, jerking violently before I can stop myself. It's the bailiff.

"Miss, let's have you exit through the side door."

I'm numb. So fucking numb. But I stand up from my seat and follow him, keeping my eyes fixed on the floor.

*Mom.*

*Dad.*

They didn't deserve this. They were innocent. I was the guilty one. I should've heeded the signs. I should've known what was coming. I should've fucking stopped him. But I was too stupid. I was too *in love*. And I have no one to blame but myself for that.

I used to think love was the answer to everything. That it was this pure and enviable thing that I could only dream of having. But now I see love for what it truly is.

*A disease.*

A sickness that infects your brain and destroys everything

in its path. And my love just might be the most insidious strain of all.

It turned Christian into a monster.

It turned me into an idiot.

And it stole every single person I've ever cared about.

My love fucking destroyed me.

And I'll never let it infect anyone else again.

# CHAPTER ONE

*Age 27, San Francisco, California*

MALE BONDING IS WEIRD AS FUCK.

I stare at Josh and watch him take another long swig of his beer as his friends Dane, Nate, and Michael, erupt in laughter at his expense. They're laughing so loud I can literally feel it in my bones, which is kind of impressive considering I'm sitting on the opposite side of the booth and there's at least a dozen flatscreens blasting a cacophony of sport sounds at us.

It's obvious Josh hates the ridicule. He's clenching his fist and his ears are turning redder and redder as their jeering stretches on, but instead of telling them to stop or trying to change the subject, he just sits there and takes it.

It's almost hard to watch.

Maybe he's a masochist?

Or has some kind of humiliation kink?

Either would be pretty surprising considering we've been on five dates and he seems as vanilla as my favorite kind of Coke.

Not that there's anything wrong with vanilla. It's comforting. Nice. Safe.

*Ugh*, why does it feel like I'm describing a cozy cottage near a lake?

We haven't even had sex yet, but I have a feeling there will be little to no orgasms in my near future.

Don't get me wrong, Josh is handsome. He has this sort of clean-cut, all-American look to him, with his sandy brownish-blonde hair and kind blue eyes that you could easily get lost in. Is he exactly my type? No. But that's probably a good thing.

As if summoned by my pessimistic thoughts, Josh reaches under the table and gives my hand a gentle squeeze.

*God,* I need to be nicer to him. Josh is a nice guy and could actually be good-for-me. Who cares if he has terrible friends and the spine of a jellyfish? At least I know he'd never hurt me. He may not be what I want, but he could be what I need. And after everything I've been through, that has to count for something.

Besides, the man practically worships the ground I walk on and has been bending over backwards to make tonight happen. I rarely do the whole "meet the friends" thing, but when he showed up at Better Than Fiction unannounced and practically begged me to come out with him and his friends after work, I didn't have the heart to tell him no.

Apparently, they've been giving him shit about making me up and that me "always being busy at my bookstore" was just an excuse to cover up his obvious lie.

While running the shop does keep me busy, I'd be lying if I said that was the only reason I've been avoiding them.

The thing is, meeting friends makes things between us more serious. And the minute things get serious, the next expectation is love.

What I feel for Josh isn't anywhere close to love, and for me, it never will be.

He says he's okay with that. That he's willing to take whatever I'll give him. But that's what everyone says before they catch feelings and the reality of my damage sinks in.

I stir my pineapple vodka and watch the four of them, feeling disconnected from the whole scene.

Josh's friends weren't very attractive to begin with, but they're all just a touch uglier when they laugh like this. It's like the features that looked a little wonky on them before, are even more pronounced now.

Dane's beady eyes are beadier.

Nate's scrunched up nose is scrunchier.

And Michael's veiny forehead is veinier.

I stop stirring my drink and freeze.

*Shit.*

Do I look uglier when I laugh, too?

*Goddamnit,* now I need to check.

After making sure they're all still deeply enthralled in their jabbing contest, I flip my compact open under the table and stare at my reflection as I discretely mimic my laughing faces.

*Okay, the nose is still nosing...*

*The teeth are still teething...*

*The eyes are still eyeing...*

"Dahlia... what are you doing?"

The sound of Josh's voice startles the hell out of me. I snap my compact shut and look up to find him and his friends staring.

"Huh?" I reply automatically, despite the fact that I definitely heard him the first time.

Josh furrows his brow. "I asked what you were doing."

I swallow and my eyes ping-pong between him and his three friends.

*Fuck, I knew coming out with them was a bad idea.*

"I uhh… thought I had something stuck in my teeth." I say, pointing vaguely to my mouth.

Josh cocks his head at me, as do his friends, and warmth rushes up neck. I try to break the awkwardness with a laugh, but Josh doesn't even crack a smile. He just stares at me.

"Beautiful and funny." Nate says, squeezing Josh's shoulder. "No wonder this poor fuck thinks you're the love of his life."

The forced smile on my face dies immediately.

*What?*

*Why the hell would he think that?*

I look around the table, and Josh's eyes cut to me so fast it makes my stomach flip. I take in Josh's expression. He doesn't look embarrassed or angry. He looks *guilty.*

The truth punches me in the face.

*Josh thinks I'm the love of his life.* We've only been on five dates and he's already there. We haven't even had sex yet, and he's already there.

*This can't be happening.*

I plaster a smile on my face and take another sip of my drink, hoping the act of normalcy will be enough to stop them from scrutinizing my reaction. It works, and their conversations continue, but it doesn't stop the panic from churning in my stomach.

I grip the edge of my seat to try to ground myself, but it's no use. And the longer I sit here, the more claustrophobic I feel. I can't breathe. I need to get out of here. *Now.*

My legs feel like they're filled with concrete as I slide out of the booth, but I force them to move, anyway.

"Doll?" Josh calls out, noticing my departure. "Where are you going?"

"Bathroom." I chirp back. He's trying to search my face, but I can't bring myself to look him in the eye.

"Let me show you where it is." He offers, already sliding his body across the pleather seat.

"I'll find it." I reply, waving a hand at him. "Stay with your friends."

Josh pauses mid-stand, and his brow furrows. "Are you sure—"

"Yeah. I'll be back."

Josh frowns as he studies my face, and I can see the muscles working in his throat. He doesn't say anything, probably because his friends are paying attention now, but his eyes are begging me not to leave. His body looks filled with tension as he watches my retreat, and I can tell it's taking all of his willpower not to chase after me.

One of his friends, Michael, I think, breaks the tension by coughing "simp" under his breath, and the others laugh again.

Josh doesn't join them. Instead, his eyes stay on me. I can feel them burning into my back, even after I turn and walk away.

# CHAPTER TWO

THE HALLWAY I'M WALKING DOWN IS NARROW AND DIMLY LIT, lined with dozens of autographed photos of celebrities I vaguely recognize. I glance at each one as I pass to help distract myself, but after a while, it starts to feel dizzying, so I give up and focus on the floor instead.

Releasing a long sigh, I massage my temples and try my hardest to rub the memory of Josh's pathetic puppy-dog face from my head.

*God,* I knew coming here was a mistake.

*Five dates.*

*Five freaking dates.*

That has to be a new record for me.

On the bright side, it's still early enough to end things without too much fallout, so I guess there's that.

I let out another long sigh.

I honestly don't even know why I bother dating anymore. I'm fundamentally incapable of giving people the one thing they're really after. And contrary to popular belief, it isn't sex that men want most, it's love, adoration, and attachment.

Sex, I can do. Sex is simpler. Sex can happen without feelings ever needing to be involved. But I'm not equipped to handle all of that other stuff, and I can't keep setting myself up for failure like this.

Maybe I just need to create a Tinder account and be completely blunt about what I can handle to save everyone the trouble.

Hey, I'm Dahlia Delacruz. I'm 27 and my hobbies include reading, watching movies, and running away at the first sign of emotional attachment. Wanna bang?

A harsh laugh spills from my lips.

*Yeah, that's a great way to attract a sociopath.*

The hallway curves to the right, and I follow it, expecting to finally find the restroom, but instead, I land in some kind of storage hallway. There's a long line of metal shelves filled with various food packaging supplies, and a bunch of liquor boxes piled against the wall.

I'm probably not supposed to be back here, and I definitely took a wrong turn somewhere, but I'm not even mad about it. The farther away from Josh and his friends, the better.

The heels of my boots click softly against the linoleum floor as I wander farther down the hall, biding my time. And before long, I reach the end of the hallway. I'm about to turn around when my eyes catch on the emergency exit. There's an empty milk crate wedged against the door, holding it open just enough to let a sliver of the back alley peek through.

*God, yes.*

Exactly what I need. An escape route I can take without having to explain myself to anyone. No awkward conversations. No evading questions. No public displays of emotion.

Before I can overthink it, I shove the door open and step outside.

The alley behind the sports bar is nearly pitch black, save for the few scattered streetlights, casting dim pools of yellow on the rain-slicked pavement.

I walk along the side of the building, or at least I think I do, but I can barely see anything beyond the silhouette of a few dumpsters and parked cars ahead of me. It's so disorienting. The alley keeps branching off into smaller, darker paths, and it feels longer and more twisted than it should.

*Jesus, it's cold tonight,* I think to myself, wrapping my bare arms across my chest for warmth. *And of course, I left my jacket in the car.*

Fuck, I think I'm lost.

I fish through my purse for my phone, and just as I'm about to pull up the navigation app, the sound of voices cuts through the silence.

*Shit.* Someone else is out here.

Chilling sounds of laughter echo in the wind and are swiftly followed by grunts of what I can only assume is pain.

*Fuck.* Someone's in trouble.

*This isn't your problem.* I think, trying to reason with myself. *No one would judge you if you walked away right now.*

*I would judge me,* I argue back, *I would blame myself for not at least trying to help.*

Deciding to follow my instincts, I follow the sounds and do everything I can to stay as hidden as possible.

Maybe it's a couple of friends play fighting. Maybe it's some drunk asshole laughing at his own stupidity. Maybe it's nothing. All of my maybes go to shit when I round the corner and find a brutal scene playing out before me.

Four men, each one bigger than the last, are attacking someone on the ground. Their feet rise and fall in a sickening rhythm, and the man's body rocks with every blow.

*Jesus.* They're going to kill him.

My instincts scream at me to run, to get the hell out of here before they notice me. But with each crack of bone on bone, my resolve grows. I can't just stand here and let them kill him. I won't. No one deserves to have their life violently stolen from them like that. No one.

"Stop it!" I shout, the words tearing out of me before I can think better of them.

All four heads snap in my direction, and their eyes narrow like predators spotting prey.

The shortest of them laughs. "You lost, little girl?"

I scan my surroundings, taking in the four massive figures, the dim lighting, and the lack of any clear escape route.

Four against one. Not great odds in general, but especially shitty when the one has heeled boots on. *Fuck.*

Running isn't an option. I have the pocket-knife Fallon got me hidden in my sock, but I've never even used it, and I know it won't be enough to scare them off. My mind races.

"Look, I-I don't want any trouble." I stutter, stepping back.

The biggest one, with a nasty scar across his cheek, advances. "Then you shouldn't have come looking for it, sweetheart."

I take another step back, eyes darting to the man on the ground. His eyes are closed, but his chest is still moving up and down. Good, he's still breathing. I silently will him to get up and run. But he just lies there. *Shit.*

"Stay back," I warn, holding my phone up like a shield, "Or I swear to God, I'll call the cops."

"Oh no, guys," the big one mocks, "guess we better leave her alone."

The others laugh as they follow behind him. My stomach

twists as their smug smiles widen. This is bad. This is really fucking bad.

The big one comes at me first, cornering me against the side of a building. He lunges for me and, without hesitation, I duck down, yank the pocket knife from my boot, and pop back up, slashing wildly.

The blade catches the side of his face and carves through his skin in a jagged slice. The wet sound he makes as his hands fly up to his bleeding face makes my stomach churn.

Shock ripples through his friends, and their laughter dies immediately. Then, without warning, they attack.

The man closest to him tries to grab me, but I twist out of his hold and use my shoulder to slam into his chest, hard. He stumbles back a step, more caught off guard than hurt, but it's enough to give me a second to prepare myself.

Another man comes for me, faster than the other two, and I wildly swing the knife in his direction. He pulls back just in time, leaving the blade to slice the air where his stomach had been a second ago.

"She fucking stabbed him!" He yells, looking between his bleeding friend and the knife in my hand.

The last man stares at me and goes to reach for the gun at his waistband. The sight of it sends pure terror ricocheting through my body. If he grabs that gun, I'm dead.

I charge him without thinking, my knife slicing at him in shallow, messy strikes. He curses at me and slams his elbow into my back, knocking the breath from my lungs and sending me tumbling forward.

As soon as I hit the ground, rough hands grab me from every direction. Ripping at anything they can get their hands on. Someone pries the knife from my grip, and before I even realize what's happening, I'm forced back on my feet, and a thick arm is wrapping around my neck and crushing my throat.

*Fuck.*

I claw at the arm choking me, kicking wildly, but my feet barely scrape the pavement as he lifts me off the ground with terrifying ease.

"Kill that bitch, Rico!" One of them shouts, tending to the first man I stabbed. "Look what she did to Aldo!"

The arm around my neck squeezes harder, and my vision starts to blur at the edges. I try to head-butt his chin, but miss, and in return, he slams my face hard against the brick wall. White explodes behind my eyes.

"You have no idea who you're fucking with," he snarls, pressing his cracked lips to my ear.

I try to kick, to fight, to do something, but my body betrays me. He has me pinned against the brick wall, and my limbs are heavy and utterly useless.

I can't breathe. I can't fucking breathe.

A deafening bang rings out, and I flinch as the sound ricochets through my entire body. The arm around my neck loosens, and the weight pressing against me eases off.

I suck in a ragged breath as I turn to face them, my eyes narrowing at the puzzling scene. The four of them are just standing there, staring at each other with wide-eyed confusion.

*What the hell is happening?*

Another bang rings out, and the man who was just choking me jerks forward. Before I can even process what's happening, his face explodes, and he collapses to the ground. Another one sounds, then another, and another, and like a twisted version of "Down the Clown" the rest of the men collapse next to him. Their bodies land with sickening thumps, and I stare, transfixed on the glistening pools of blood stretching across the pavement beneath them.

I slowly look back up, and the sight in front of me makes me audibly gasp.

The man they were beating is now standing. He's tall, at least a foot or more above me. Maybe somewhere around 6'5 or 6'6. There's a gun in his hand and a gnarly gash above his brow. Blood streaks down the side of his face, sliding against the hollow of his cheeks before catching on the edge of his clenched jaw. He stares at me through the dark strands of hair hanging over his eyes, and I can't help but stare back.

He's stupidly pretty for a killer.

Full brows, dark eyes, and the kind of panty-melting bone structure you can stare at for hours. He has tattoos crawling up the side of his neck, half hidden by the collar of his white shirt, and despite the blood and the gun and the four bodies at his feet, he looks completely unfazed.

He takes a step towards me, and I flinch back, pressing myself harder into the brick. I'm trying to stay calm, but my body is acting purely on instinct. It's as if it can sense the danger I'm in and has shifted into pure self-preservation mode.

As he inches closer, his eyes stay on mine, then dip lower for a second too long, before lazily lifting back up.

I glance down at myself.

*Shit.*

One of the straps on my dress is torn, and the neckline is pulled down and stretched from where their hands grabbed at me. I didn't wear a bra today, and my breasts are almost completely exposed.

I jerk my arms up immediately, yanking the fabric back into place, and trying to cover myself as best I can. When I look back up, I find him watching.

The muscles in his jaw flex, and then he slides his gun into the waistband of his pants.

My grip tightens on the fabric as my brain scrambles, every instinct screaming at me all at once. *What is he doing?*

He starts to take off his jacket, and I freeze.

*He's just as bad as they are,* a voice in the back of my head whispers. *He's worse. You misread the situation. You saved a monster.*

He strips the jacket off, and I just stand there trembling, bracing for something I can't even force myself to think about. Then, without warning, he tosses it at me.

The jacket flies in my direction, and I barely manage to catch it before it falls to the ground. For a moment, I just stand there staring at the warm pile of burgundy fabric clenched in my hands.

"Put it on." He says, sounding almost annoyed.

I hesitate, only because my brain hasn't fully caught up to what's happening, then quickly throw it on.

The jacket is heavier than I expected, and as the warm fabric settles over my shoulders, heat seeps in almost immediately. It smells faintly of smoke and a warm, woody fragrance. Something subtle but unmistakably expensive. The feel of his jacket draped over me is grounding in a way that doesn't make sense.

My breathing calms down a little, and when I look up, he's watching me again.

He stares at me for a moment, studying my face, then, ever so slowly, he pulls his gun from his waistband, levels it at my head, and smirks as he says, "This is the part where you run."

# CHAPTER THREE

Echo

THE SECOND SHE BOLTS, EVERY NERVE IN MY BODY SNAPS TO attention.

I expected her to panic. It's what people normally do when they're staring down the barrel of my gun. They beg, they shake, they scream. But not this girl.

*No.*

In that split second before she took off, she glared at me and I saw challenge in her eyes.

*Good.*

I'm not one to turn down an easy kill, but it's so much more interesting to play with your food before you eat it.

It's why the situation with the Casello's men got so out of hand.

A week ago, my brother and I came to an agreement with Dante Casello. The Italians would stop encroaching on our territory and ports. And in return, The Sannikovs would stop leaving bodies for them to find.

I didn't like having my hands tied, but it was a necessary

evil to keep our business in order, so I agreed. That is, until these four assholes crossed the line tonight.

Twenty minutes ago these motherfuckers snuck into our club and manhandled our baby sister, thinking we couldn't do anything about it.

*Stupid bastards.*

We agreed to no deaths, but no one said anything about shattering bones. The only reason I let them land a few hits first was because I wanted to be able to argue self-defense, on the off chance Casello caught wind of the altercation.

Everything was going according to plan until *she* got involved. She distracted me, allowing one of those assholes to get a clean kick in that knocked me out cold.

When I came to and realized what they were doing to her, I snapped. I don't even remember reaching for my gun. One minute it was tucked into my waistband, the next it was firing off rounds with lethal precision.

I let out a breath and take stock of the damage.

My knuckles ache, and my ribs feel like someone took a bat to them. I taste iron every time I swallow, and I can already feel my eye swelling shut.

*What a fucking mess.*

Leaning against the brick, I watch her flee and can't help but smirk at the sight of her clumsy escape. Her legs buckle underneath her and her arms flail, like a baby deer taking its first steps in the world.

*Jesus.*

*She's almost making this too easy.*

"Careful, Bambi. You might fall and snap your own neck before I get the chance to."

I could easily catch her right now.

I probably should, given the circumstances.

But the urge to end this quickly feels… distant.

*I've got this under control.*

*What's the harm in drawing it out a little?*

As soon as her silhouette disappears into the shadows, I push off the wall and begin my hunt. My shoes barely make a sound as I follow her path, my senses heightening with every step.

A trace of her scent lingers in the air. Peach tinged with the sweet smell of desperation.

"Come out, come out, wherever you are."

I round a sharp edge of a building and spot her just a few yards ahead. She glances back, eyes wide, hair wild.

"Run faster. Unless, of course, you want to get caught."

"Fuck off, psycho!" She screams, pushing herself to run even faster.

The fire in her voice only fuels my drive.

She stumbles over a crack and catches herself against a dumpster before pushing off it with a grunt. She veers left, desperately trying to lose me, but I'm already two steps ahead of her. Cutting her off and herding her exactly where I want her.

She skids to a stop in front of a chain-link fence and turns to face me, her back slamming against it. The metal rattles, and her fingers claw at the links, searching for an exit that doesn't exist.

I slowly step towards her, my shadow swallowing hers inch by inch.

She's shorter than I expected. 5'5, 5'6 max. And the top of her head barely reaches my chest. Her face is flushed, and her brown, almond-shaped eyes are wide with panic.

"Gotcha." I murmur, lifting my gun and aiming the barrel at the center of her forehead.

"Shit." She says, dropping her hands from the fence.

"Shit indeed." I say, cocking my head. "Any last words, beautiful?"

She looks up at me then, and something in my chest misfires.

"Yeah." She says quietly, nodding her head. "Thank you."

My brows pull together. "For what?"

"For back there." She says, nodding in the direction we came from. "You saved me from whatever those men were about to do to me." She explains. "If I'm going to die tonight, I'd rather it be by your gun than their hands."

Her words register, and my jaw instantly tightens.

*People don't thank me.*

They fear me. They hate me. They survive me, if they're lucky. But they don't fucking thank me.

"I'm ready." She whispers, squeezing her eyes shut. "Just do it quickly."

I take a step closer and place my finger on the trigger, but the idea of pulling it doesn't feel clean. It feels *wrong*. Not morally, I lost that metric long ago, but viscerally.

*Who is this girl?*

First, she tries to take on four grown men all by herself. Then she stares down the barrel of my gun and fucking thanks me.

"What's wrong with you?"

It isn't what I mean to say, not in the slightest, but the words are out before I can stop them.

Her brow furrows, but her eyes stay shut. "What?"

"You accept your death so easily. Why?"

She flicks her eyes open and looks at me like there's something wrong with me. As if I'm the one thanking the person who's about to kill them.

Her mouth opens, but no sound comes out, and I've never been more aware of someone's silence.

"Do you have a death wish?"

"What?"

"Suicidal tendencies?"

Outrage flashes across her face. "That's not something to joke about."

"I'm not joking." I say flatly. "Answer the question."

"No," she hisses, squaring her shoulders. "Of course not."

"Could've fooled me."

She glares at me like she wants to stab something. Preferably me. "What are you talking about?"

"You're reckless." I say evenly. "You should've stayed out of it. Most people would have."

She narrows her eyes at me. "They were going to kill you."

"And?"

She flushes, frustration carving lines into her delicate features. "And I couldn't just—" She cuts herself off. Re-centers. "I couldn't just leave you there to die."

*Why the hell would she try to protect me?*

No one does that. No one steps between someone and danger. No one takes a hit meant for someone else. I do, but only because I was raised to do that. For River. For Athena. For Briggs. For the people closest to me, but never for some fucking stranger in an alley.

I stare at her, unsure of what to do next.

I eliminate threats. It's what I'm good at, what I fucking excel at. And despite what she saw, she still doesn't feel like a threat to me.

*So why the fuck would I kill her?*

Before I even track that I'm doing it, I lower my gun and tuck it back into my waistband.

Her eyes flick to the movement, then back to me. "You

aren't going to—" She says, cutting herself off like she's scared to say the rest of the words out loud.

"I'm not going to kill you. As misguided as your actions were, you were trying to save me. So I'm willing to entertain other solutions."

Relief hits her so hard, she nearly doubles over.

"But." I add, because there's always a but. "We're still at an impasse here, Bambi. You saw what I did. I can't just let you walk away."

"Why not?"

I tilt my head.

"You'll talk, and we both know I'm too pretty to go to jail."

She glares at me, but I can tell she's fighting the urge to smile by the way her lips twitch.

"I promise I won't." She says softly. "And as far as I'm concerned, what happened back there was self-defense."

"Self-defense." I repeat slowly.

"Yes."

"I killed four men without a second thought."

She swallows. "I know, but they deserved it. They nearly killed you and were in the middle of attacking me. If anything, you saved me."

This isn't how these situations usually play out. People see the monster and they run screaming. They don't stand there arguing semantics and morality.

"Look." She says, pulling me from my thoughts. "I won't talk, I swear. Can we just go our separate ways and pretend like tonight never happened?"

Her idea doesn't sit well with me. It doesn't even register as possible. I shake my head. "A promise isn't going to cut it, Bambi."

She furrows her brow, and there's almost something

scientific about the expression that takes over her face. She looks like she's been given a complex problem and is trying her damnedest to solve it.

"The knife." She says suddenly, looking up at me. "The one I used on them. It has my prints all over it and their blood. You could keep it as leverage. Then we'd both be in trouble if I talked."

*Smart girl.*

"Good." I say, crossing my arms. "But still not enough. Those men weren't just anybody, and the cops aren't the only ones I need to be concerned about."

She tries again, desperation tightening her features. "What if you check up on me?" She offers. "You know, make sure I stay quiet. We could… keep in touch. Like friends."

*Friends.*

She says it like it's harmless. Like she isn't offering me a way into every unguarded part of her life.

Friendship gives me proximity without the complication of resistance. It gives me permission. A reason to ask questions. A reason to watch.

I stare at her for a moment, letting the silence stretch. Watching the way her shoulders tense and the way she still hasn't looked away, despite the fear threading through her.

"You want to be my friend." I say slowly, tasting the word on my tongue.

Her mouth twitches. "I want to walk out of here alive. If staying in contact with you is what makes that happen, then so be it."

Honest, desperate, yet extraordinarily calculated.

I look at her for a long moment. Long enough that her breathing changes. Long enough that I can see the exact moment she starts to question if she's going to survive this.

"Alright."

Her eyes widen. "Really?"

"Yes. But if you lie to me, if you disappear, or if I even get the sense that you're thinking about talking to anyone—"

She swallows. "I won't."

I nod. "Give me your phone."

She hesitates for half a second before handing it over. She already knows there's no point in arguing.

I fire off a quick text to myself before handing it back to her and pulling out my own cell.

"What's your real name, Bambi?" I ask, locking eyes with her.

"Dahlia." She whispers, lowering her gaze to her phone before glancing back up at me. "What's yours?"

"Echo," I reply, stepping back and giving her space I don't intend to respect for long.

"It's… nice to meet you, Echo." She says hesitantly. "Thank you for letting me go."

I cock my head at her. "Who says I have?"

She swallows, blinking her eyes hard. "But you said…" She drifts off.

"Leave." I whisper, fighting a smile as I watch fear rake through her. "Before I change my mind."

She doesn't need to be told twice. She slides past me, and her shoulder brushes against mine for the briefest moment before she disappears into the night.

I stand there for a minute, watching the space she left behind.

I'm sure Bambi thinks this ends here. That she negotiated her safety and she'll never have to see me again. But she's wrong.

We're friends now.

And I intend to be there for her.

Whether she likes it or not.

# CHAPTER FOUR

*Dahlia*

Smoke hangs low in the bathroom, curling along the walls and distorting the edges of the room until everything feels just a little out of focus. I sit in the bath, staring up at the ceiling, trying to calm my breathing.

*You're okay.*

*You're safe now.*

I try not to think about why the heaviness in my chest feels so familiar, but the unwelcome thought slips through, anyway.

*The last time you felt like this, you had just lost everyone. You sat in a tub just like this, staring at bruises that hadn't finished blooming, wondering if you'd ever be okay again.*

What the hell was I thinking?

I've carefully designed my life to avoid this feeling. My nights are quiet. My mornings are peaceful. And the bookstore keeps my mind busy during the day so thoughts of the past stay deep in the recesses of my mind. But now, it's all floating up to the fucking surface, no matter how hard I try to press them back down.

Pulling the blunt up to my lips again, I take another long hit and sink deeper into the tub, letting the sweet numbness wash over me.

*God,* I needed this.

The quiet.

The nothingness.

The peace.

It's a jarring contrast to the hell that was tonight, and now that my adrenaline has run its course, the reality of what happened is hitting me hard.

I stare down at my battered body beneath the water and feel myself getting choked up at the sight of it. *I knew it was bad.* The pain on the drive home warned me as much. But it's the first time I'm getting a real look at the damage, and it's so much worse than I thought.

The bruises on my neck don't surprise me. I could feel the pressure lingering there, long after he let me go. But the bruises all over my arms and torso were something I didn't expect. I remember feeling their rough hands grab at me, I guess I just didn't realize how violently they did it.

I gently run my fingers across the tender red and purple blotches.

*You could've died tonight.*

At that thought, my mind slips back to the alley. To the men who attacked me, to their blood on the concrete and then, inevitably, to *him.*

When Echo raised his gun at me, there was no confusion about what it meant. No pretending. No lies meant to distract me from the truth. He made it clear I was in danger and that he would pull the trigger if he wanted to.

Christian always hid his danger from me. He covered it up with soft words, pretty promises, and a smile that convinced you to ignore the warning signs until it was too late.

Echo didn't hide anything from me. He was honest in the ugliest way, and I think a small part of me respects that. Even if he is a psychotic killer.

I'm not sure how much time passes as I sit there contemplating my mortality, but by the time a knock on the door pulls me out of my trance, the temperature of the water has plummeted and my fingers and toes have thoroughly pruned.

"Hey D," Fallon calls out, her voice muffled through the door. "Can I come in? I really have to pee."

I glance at the door, then at the blunt perched on the edge of the tub. *Her* blunt.

*Shit.*

"I'll be right out." I stammer, stubbing the blunt out in the ashtray and pulling myself out of the now freezing water.

My eyes dart to Echo's jacket, still draped over the sink where I left it. If Fallon sees it, I know she'll have questions.

I lunge for it, nearly slipping on the wet tile, and shove it under my pile of clothes before quickly wrapping a towel around myself and heading for the door.

"Sorry." I say, shielding my face as I crack the door open. "I kind of lost track of time in there."

"All good." She says, shouldering past me, with her honey blonde hair swinging behind her. "If it weren't an emergency, I totally wouldn't have cared."

Fallon isn't just my roommate. She's my best friend and the person who dragged me out of my wreckage and refused to let me disappear when I lost my parents eleven years ago. She's the closest thing I have to family now, and she will absolutely lose her shit if she finds out what I did tonight.

Fallon unbuttons her jeans, and I turn my back to her as I take a seat on the edge of the tub. I'm trying to act normal, but it's hard to pretend like I'm not hyper-aware of the bruises I'm hiding from her, so I wipe the condensation off the faucet, just to give my hands something to do.

Fallon finishes her business and glides across the tile to wash her hands in the sink. After she's done, she glances up and completely freezes when she catches my reflection in the mirror.

"D, what the fuck?" She asks, shutting off the faucet and whipping around to face me.

My eyes burn, but I fix my gaze back on the tub. "What?"

Fallon crosses the bathroom in two long strides, cups my chin, and angles my face toward the light. Her fingers are gentle, but her grip is firm, and I can tell she's trying to hold in her anger.

"Jesus," she breathes, studying my face. "What happened?"

"I'm fine," I say automatically. "It looks worse than it feels."

"Bullshit," she replies flatly.

I try to pull back, but she doesn't let me. Her eyes track the cuts along my cheekbone and the marks on my neck. The concern on her face hurts worse than the pain does.

"Who did this?" She asks, her voice suddenly sounding eerily calm. "Spill, Dahlia. Now."

*Fuck.*

"I got mugged." I lie.

Fallon's brows knit together. "What?"

"It was stupid," I add quickly. "I shouldn't have fought back. I was outside alone in a shitty part of town and some guys tried to rob me."

"You're sure thats all?" She asks, her voice sounding softer now, almost wistful.

I swallow and nod, grateful that at least that part is true.

"Luckily, a guy stepped in to stop them, but not before one asshole slammed my face into a wall. I'm fine, though. It's not a big deal."

Her mouth tightens. "That is a big deal."

"I would've told you," I say. "I just didn't want you to worry. Honestly, I just wanted to take a bath and pretend like it never happened."

Fallon assesses me for a moment, searching my face. Words are on the tip of her tongue. I can feel them there, ready to leap out and prod at me.

"Sit," she says, releasing my chin before moving toward the medicine cabinet above the sink.

"You really don't need to do all that."

"Yes, I do," she cuts in, rifling through supplies with single-minded focus.

I lower myself onto the edge of the tub and slowly shake my head.

*I knew she'd freak out.*

Fallon comes back with a small first-aid kit and a bottle of alcohol. She douses a cotton pad in it and presses it against my cheek.

I suck in a breath and wince.

"Fucker," she mutters with a smirk. "I knew you were lying about it not hurting."

I stare down at the towel wrapped around my body as my fingers play with the hem.

"Did you call the cops?" She asks.

"No."

"Dahlia."

"I didn't want to deal with it," I say, because the truth is more complicated. "I just wanted to come home."

Fallon's jaw clenches and I can tell she's pissed. Not at

me. At the world. She's always been like this. Loud and bossy while still being impossibly warm.

Fallon St. James is objectively hot. Not only is she unfairly pretty, but she also has a naturally toned body that most women would kill to have. At first glance, most people think she's a bitch, purely because she won the genetic lottery. But that couldn't be further from the truth.

Fallon is the kindest person I know. And despite her somewhat prickly exterior, she cares deeply for others and is always willing to fight for what she believes in.

It's one of the reasons I love her. It's also one of the reasons I lie. Because if she knew the truth about tonight, she'd burn the world down trying to protect me. And I can't survive losing another person because of my own stupid choices.

She reaches for a bandage and pauses, her gaze flicking to the edge of the tub.

Fallon's brows lift. "Uh… are you smoking my weed?"

Heat rushes up my neck. "No."

Fallon stares at me.

"Okay." I exhale. "Yes. Technically. I am."

"Technically," she repeats, deadpan.

"It was a rough night."

Fallon snorts, shaking her head as she goes back to tending to my face. I can tell she's relieved, though she's trying her best to hide it.

"Alright. Stay here." She says, stepping back to assess her work. "I'm going to grab an ice pack from the freezer."

She disappears, and I sit there in the quiet, with my towel still twisted in my hands.

I should be thinking about the mugger lie and how I'm going to keep it straight if Fallon asks questions tomorrow. Instead, my mind slides back to Echo.

To the way he looked at me. To the way he said, very plainly, that he couldn't let me walk away.

*But he did, didn't he?* At least, I hope he did.

A moment later, Fallon returns with an ice pack wrapped in a dish towel and tosses it to me.

"Hold it," she orders.

I do.

She leans against the counter, watching me with a look that is equal parts annoyance and care. "You're going to bed," she says. "And tomorrow, we'll reassess. If you wake up dizzy or nauseous, I'm taking you to urgent care, and you will not fight me on it."

"I wasn't going to fight."

Fallon arches a brow.

"Okay. I probably would've."

"Exactly, bitch." She replies playfully. "Don't forget I know you."

I laugh, pressing the ice against my cheek as I stare at the tiled floor.

"I'm glad you're okay."

My throat tightens. "I am, too."

She gives me a nod, then points to the blunt still perched on the edge of the tub. "Also, if your square ass is going to smoke some of my weed, at least have the decency to invite me to join in. You never smoke with me." She pouts.

I huff a laugh and shake my head.

"Next time. I promise."

Fallon's blue eyes sparkle with mischief. "Shut up! Are you saying there's going to be a next time? Dahlia Delacruz, don't you play with my emotions right now."

"Goodnight, Fallon." I say, fighting a smile as I practically shove her towards the door.

"I'm holding you to it, fucker." She grumbles, stomping

out into the hallway. "Head injury or not, a promise is a freaking promise."

The door shuts behind her, and my eyes drift to the counter, to where my phone has been sitting face-down for the last few hours.

I tell myself I only want to check it out of habit. Or boredom. Or because tonight is finally over and I'm trying to anchor myself in something normal.

But when I flip it over and see his name lighting up my screen, the fact that I immediately open his message, tells me I'm full of shit.

Echo: Did you get home okay?

It's such a simple question. Normal, even. The kind of thing a friend would ask.

Except, we're not friends. Not really. And the fact that he's already checking in on me. Already inserting himself into my life like he has every right to be there, is a fucking problem.

I don't know what he wants from me, but it's clear whatever this is between us isn't over. It's just getting started.

# CHAPTER FIVE

*Echo*

There's a special place in hell for people with an exorbitant amount of wealth. And tonight, our club is filled to the brim with them.

Billionaires. Founders. CEOs. Board Members.

They all flock to this place like it's their fucking house of worship. And I suppose, in a lot of ways, it is. Only, there are no gods that roam these dimly lit spaces, only devils. And the only ones being worshipped here are them.

Question.

*What does one offer to someone who has everything they could want?*

Answer.

*Every fucking thing they can't.*

Our club provides a service.

These rich assholes pay to play in our space and in turn, we take extra precautions to make sure that their deepest fucked-up desires never see the light of day.

Oracle is the one place where they can lower their carefully crafted masks. The one place where every single person in their vicinity has their own secrets to protect.

Harry, our head bartender, notices me approaching the bar and immediately sets down the glass he's drying. He pours a double shot of vodka and wordlessly slides it over.

I take a long sip and let the weight of tonight's decisions settle over me. Four of Casello's men are dead. That doesn't come without consequences.

From the corner of my eye, I catch one of our newer waitresses whispering to another. Her eyes flick towards me, and when she notices me looking, she immediately averts her gaze and walks in the opposite direction.

My jaw ticks.

They all think I'm unstable. That I'm a monster with a mean streak and a propensity for violence. They're not wrong. Still, it would be nice for my reputation not to precede me everywhere I go.

I drain the rest of my glass and am just about to signal to Harry to pour me another, when I sense someone coming up behind me.

"Echo, thank god!" Athena exclaims, looping her arms around me. She pulls back and studies me for a moment, concern shining in her hazel eyes.

Earlier tonight flashes through my mind. Athena at the bar, laughing with some friends. Those four assholes backing her into a corner by herself. The look of terror on my baby sister's face.

Athena reaches her hand towards the cut above my brow. I cleaned up before coming back here, but it's probably still noticeable. "What happened?"

"Nothing." I say dismissively. "Just a work thing."

Her brow furrows, and I can tell she wants me to say more, but she doesn't press.

At twenty-six, she's only two years younger than me and four years younger than River, our older brother, but he and I make it a point to protect her from the more gruesome details of our family business. She wasn't raise for it like we were, so she's used to getting non-answers from us.

"Well, I'm just glad you're okay."

I cock my head at her. "Why wouldn't I be?"

She tucks a strand of wavy brown hair behind her ear and leans in closer. "Security found bodies in the back alley." Her voice drops to a whisper. "When you didn't answer my calls… I thought—"

"You thought I could be one of them." I finish.

Athena nods, her expression tight. "Apparently, they were unrecognizable."

*Yeah.*

*Close-range shots to the head will do that to you.*

"Where's River?"

"In the office with Briggs." She sighs. "As soon as word came in, they freaked and practically shoved me out."

"I'll talk to them." I glance over her shoulder and give a subtle nod to her security. They close in around her before she can protest.

"Tread lightly." She warns. "River looked ready to kill someone."

I take the stairs two at a time. The music fades into a low pulse behind me. Upstairs, the office door is open. River is pacing back and forth, tension etched into every step. And Briggs, our right hand man and childhood best friend, is leaning against the wall with his arms crossed, looking lost in thought.

I step in and shut the door behind me.

"Where the fuck have you been?" River asks, his dark

eyes skimming over the fresh cuts on my face. "And why the hell haven't you been answering your phone?"

"I was occupied."

River's eyes narrow. "You don't happen to know anything about the bodies we found outside, do you?"

I shrug, crossing the room and dropping onto the leather couch. "Should I?"

River stops pacing and turns to face me, his eyes cutting through the dim light of the office.

"Don't play dumb, Echo. You go missing, and thirty minutes later, four of Casello's men are dead. You expect me to believe that's a coincidence?"

I meet his gaze, my expression neutral. "Coincidences happen."

Briggs pushes off the wall, walks to the bar, and pours himself a drink. "Where were you tonight?"

"Out." I reply cooly, leaning back and stretching my arms over my head. "I needed some air."

The room falls silent save for the sound of the ice clinking in Briggs's glass.

Neither of them believe me. That much is obvious.

"You know how delicate the ceasefire is." Briggs warns. "If Casello finds out we had something to do with his men's disappearance—"

"He won't."

River curses under his breath as he pinches the bridge of his nose. "What the hell were you thinking? What if someone saw you out there?"

*Someone did.*

But he doesn't need to know that.

"Did we sweep for surveillance?" River asks, directing the question to Briggs.

"Yeah." Briggs replies, taking a slow sip of his bourbon.

"No cameras on that stretch. We cleared what little footage existed of the area."

"Then there's nothing to worry about." I say.

River glares at me. "You still haven't told us what the hell happened. Why did you go after them?"

Neither of them knows what happened to Athena tonight. If they did, this conversation would look very different, and we'd have an all-out war on our hands. Both of them are even more protective of her than I am.

"I needed to blow off some steam." I say. "And things escalated."

River looks at me the same way he always does. Like he's trying to find the piece of me he can fix and keeps coming up empty. I've told him that what happened when we were kids wasn't his fault. That I was raised to be the weapon, he was raised to be the hand that wields it, and neither of us had a say in the matter. Still, I can tell it haunts him every time he looks at me.

River lets out a tired sigh and waves his hand.

"Let's just focus on cleaning this up before Casello starts sniffing around."

Briggs nods. "Our guys are working on it now. The scene will be pristine within the hour."

"You sure no one saw what happened?" River asks.

I hold his stare, knowing this is a line I'm intentionally crossing.

"Positive."

He nods and takes a seat behind his desk, already attending to his next order of business.

I push off the couch and head for the door, eager to get away from the mess I know I'm making.

The second I'm in the hallway, I pull out my phone. The text I sent an hour ago still sits there, unanswered.

Echo: Did you get home okay?

I tap the screen, checking the delivery receipt. It went through. She has her phone, I'm sure she's seen it.

Given our arrangement, I assumed she'd respond immediately. She should be eager to comply and desperate to stay on my good side, but she isn't responding.

*Interesting.*

My message wasn't invasive or threatening. If anything, it was friendly. So why does her silence feel like the first sign of resistance?

My jaw tightens.

I lock the screen and slide the phone back into my pocket. She can't ignore me forever. I'll make sure of it.

# CHAPTER SIX

THE DOOR CHIMES AND I GLANCE UP AUTOMATICALLY, expecting to see another customer walk through the door.

Instead, it's the last person I expected to see.

*Echo.*

It's been over a week since that night in the alley. In the time since, I half convinced myself I imagined him. That he was just some kind of scary hot apparition my brain created after being under severe duress.

But nope.

He's real. And he's standing in the doorway of my bookstore looking even more attractive in the daylight.

He's dressed in all black. Wearing a fitted t-shirt that does nothing to hide the muscles underneath it and a pair of jeans that sit low on his hips and are way too tight around his—

*Nope.*

Not going there.

His dark hair is combed back neatly, and there's a faint shadow of stubble along his jaw. A man like him has no business looking this hot.

Nature is kind of twisted in that way. It's like the universe purposely makes the most dangerous things alluring just to fuck with us.

He steps further in, letting the door swing shut behind him, and every other customer in Better Than Fiction notices. Their heads swivel in his direction cartoonishly, and my eyes flare when a woman standing near the historical romance section actually bites her lip when she spots him.

*Jesus.*

He's pretty, but he's not that pretty.

And if they had any idea what he was capable of, eye-fucking him would be the last thing on their minds.

He walks up to me with his hands in his pockets, looking entirely too comfortable in my space. Those dark amber eyes track over me slowly, taking inventory, and I feel completely exposed despite the fact that I'm fully clothed. Having him here, in my carefully controlled space, is making every single one of my nerve endings fire all at once.

*How the fuck did he find me?*

"What are you doing here?" I manage, narrowing my eyes at him, as I flash him my fakest customer service smile.

He tilts his head and smirks as if he finds my reaction amusing. "You never answered my text."

My smile drops and I press my lips together. "What?"

"Did you get home okay?" He explains, his voice low. "The night we met. I asked. You never answered."

My throat tightens, and I glare at him. "That was over a week ago." I hiss.

"I know." His eyes linger on my face, cataloging every detail. "I still want my answer. So, did you get home okay?"

I stare at him and try to pretend like my stomach isn't flipping in on itself.

"I did." I say tightly, crossing my arms over my chest. "As you can see."

The defensive posture does nothing to help. If anything, it just makes me more aware of how close he is and how much bigger he is than me.

He takes another step closer, and his eyes catch on my cheekbone. On the fading bruise I spent twenty minutes covering with concealer this morning.

"You're covering it with makeup."

"Yeah." I say quickly. "But it's mostly healed."

"Show me."

I take a step back. "Excuse me?"

"The bruises." He says, his voice calm and almost conversational. "The ones they gave you. The ones you're covering with a turtleneck in the middle of August. I want to see them."

Heat crawls up my neck. "No. Absolutely not."

"Why not?"

"Because this is a business." I hiss, grasping for any excuse that creates distance. "And you're a customer. You can't just—"

He moves.

One minute he's on the other side of the counter. The next, he's rounding it and backing me against the shelves behind the register.

"Echo—"

His hand comes up to my face and I freeze. He trails his fingers down the side of my face, and his touch is so gentle and so unexpected that it makes my breath catch. His thumb ghosts over the fading bruise on my cheek, and when I tense up, something dark flashes in his eyes.

"It still hurts." He murmurs, more to himself than to me.

I need to push him away. I need to tell him to get the fuck

out of my store. Instead, I'm rooted in place, watching him touch me as my heart pounds erratically in my chest.

His fingers slide down and slowly trace the side of my neck, coming to a pause on the edge of my turtleneck. He swallows as his eyes bore into the black fabric around my neck, then, ever-so-slowly, he tugs it down to reveal the marks there.

The bruises have faded to a sickly yellowish-green, but they're still visible. Still a reminder of how close I came to dying that night. His jaw tightens as he traces them with his fingers.

"They put their hands on you here, too." It's not a question.

I swallow hard, and he feels it beneath his fingers. "They did—"

"I should've made it slower." He whispers. His thumb presses gently against my pulse point, and I know he can feel how fast my heart is racing. "I should've made them suffer more for what they did to you."

The violence in his voice should scare me.

It doesn't though, and I can't explain why.

"They're dead." I whisper. "That's enough."

His eyes meet mine, and the intensity in them steals my breath. They're a deep amber green, and up this close I can see the flecks of gold in his irises.

"No." He says softly, his voice rough. "It's not."

I'm painfully aware of how close he is. How I can feel the heat emanating off his body in waves. And how he smells exactly like the jacket I still haven't thrown away. Woody, warm, and incredibly masculine.

I study his face, and my eyes catch on the fresh scar above his eyebrow. It's a stark reminder that we both didn't leave that night unscathed.

"You should step back." I manage, but my voice comes out breathy. *Weak.*

"Should I?" He asks, his thumb still on my neck, still feeling every frantic beat.

"Yes." I say, but even I can hear that there's no conviction in my voice.

Echo doesn't move. He just keeps looking at me like he's trying to memorize every detail.

"Your pulse is racing, Bambi."

"That's because you're scaring me."

"Liar."

My breath catches because he's right.

I'm not scared.

I'm something else entirely. And given the fact that I know what he's capable of, that's really fucking disturbing.

A throat clears behind us, and we both turn to see a woman in her 70s standing at the other side of the counter. She's clutching a book to her chest and looking deeply uncomfortable as a blush spreads across her cheeks.

Echo steps back smoothly, as if he wasn't just invading every inch of my personal space, and steps towards one of the bookshelves.

I know how intense that felt to me. I can only imagine what it looked like to her.

I ring her up quickly and am eternally grateful for her silence as she hands me her card and I slip her receipt into her bag.

She turns around, and Echo stupidly, ridiculously gives her a wink as he waves her goodbye. The poor woman literally gasps and stumbles over herself as she heads for the door.

I cut my eyes at Echo and follow her out, just to make sure she makes it to her car okay. She does, and when she slips into the driver's seat and I see the huge smile on her face, I can't help but find what Echo did a little endearing.

I step back into the store, looking for the menace, and surprisingly, I find him browsing in one of the aisles.

"What are you doing?" I ask, studying him warily.

"Shopping." He says, his voice returning to that casual tone. But when he glances at me, there's something heated in his eyes that makes my stomach flutter.

*This is insane.*

He moves to the paranormal romance section, and I feel myself following him. I watch him, completely off-balance, with my hand pressed to the side of my face that still feels the phantom of his touch.

"You don't strike me as much of a reader." I say, trying to regain some control over the situation.

He glances back over his shoulder. "You don't know me well enough to make that assumption, Bambi."

There's that nickname again.

"Don't call me that." I mutter, tugging on my collar.

"Why not?" He asks, his eyes still skimming across the shelf. "It suits you."

I grimace. "It really doesn't."

"Agree to disagree."

He pulls a book from the shelf and holds it up. "Ah, here we go. I've been looking for this one."

It's Darkfever by Karen Marie Moning.

I stare at him.

"You have?" I ask, fighting a smile.

"Yes." He says automatically. "It's been on my list for a while now."

"Hmm." I nod, trying to hide my amusement. "I didn't take you for someone into fae smut, but I'm not one to kink shame."

He quirks a brow. "Fae what—"

I watch him glance down at the cover and then look around the store. Taking in the predominantly female clientele and the shelves labeled with different genres of romance and something like realization crosses his face.

"Well, I guess it's not just fae smut." I continue with a completely straight face. "There's also these really hot mysterious beasts. And immortals. So many yummy immortals. It's one of my favorites."

Echo shakes his head and smirks at me. "Well, if it's one of your favorites." He says, drawing out his words before gently licking his lips. "Then I'm definitely taking it."

My eyes linger on his mouth for a second too long and *of course,* he notices.

"Come ring me up." He says, nodding towards the register.

I clear my throat and follow him, inwardly cursing myself for getting caught staring. Echo stops in front of the counter and slides the paperback towards me.

"You're really going to buy that?" I ask, the disbelief in my voice clear as day.

"Of course." He says smoothly, pulling a leather wallet out of his back pocket. "The books are for sale, aren't they?"

I roll my eyes and scan the book, hyper-aware that his eyes are on me.

"That'll be $16.41." I say, proud that my voice sounds at least somewhat normal.

He takes out a hundred-dollar bill, and when he hands it to me, his fingers deliberately brush against mine.

My body jolts in response.

"Jumpy." He notes, studying my face with that infuriating smirk.

I snap my hand back. "I am not."

I count out his change quickly, fumbling with the bills. My hands are shaking, and I know he notices because his mouth curves into a half-smile.

I jerk the bills toward him.

"Keep it." He says.

I wrinkle my nose. "What? No. I can't—"

"Is that not a tip jar?" He nods toward the empty glass container on the counter, but his eyes never leave my face.

I bite the inside of my cheek.

*It is.*

Unfortunately.

I clench my jaw and drop the change inside. "Thank you." I mutter.

I reach for the book to bag it, and he does too. Our fingers touch again. This time, neither of us pulls back right away.

His hands are warm and rough, with scarred knuckles that hint at the violence I know he's capable of. It's hard to believe they're the same hands that touched my face so delicately.

I feel him watching me again. Studying me.

"Did you need anything else?" I ask, trying to regain some semblance of professionalism.

"Actually, yes." He says, leaning against the counter. "I was curious about something."

"What?" I ask warily.

"Why romance?"

My brow furrows. "What do you mean?"

"This." He says, gesturing around the shop. "Why did you open a romance bookstore specifically?"

It's a normal question. The kind strangers ask when they're making small talk. But coming from him, it feels invasive. Like he's searching for something to use against me.

The real answer is that romance novels were the only

thing that made me feel something after I lost my parents. Their happily-ever-afters felt like proof that good things could still exist in my world, even if I was just experiencing them vicariously.

"I like them." I say simply.

"That's not a real answer."

"It's the only one I have for you."

His eyes narrow slightly, like he's deciding whether to push. Then they drop to my neck again.

"Your pulse is still racing."

My face flushes. "It's time for you to leave."

"Is it?" He picks up the book, tucking it under his arm, but he doesn't move away. "Or do you just need me to leave before you do something you'll regret?"

I narrow my eyes at the accusation.

I hate that there's truth in it. Hate that my body is betraying me. That some traitorous part of me likes him being here.

"You're delusional." I hiss.

He leans in, close enough that I can feel his minty breath against my ear. "Then why haven't you told me to fuck off yet?"

*Because I can't seem to form words when you're this close. Because my brain short-circuits every time you look at me like that. Because some damaged part of me recognizes the danger in you and gravitates toward it anyway.*

"I'm telling you now." I force out. "Fuck off, Echo."

His smile widens. "I love the way you say my name."

He straightens, finally putting some distance between us, but it still doesn't feel like enough. He heads for the door, and for a moment I think I'm free. Then he pauses at the threshold and turns to face me.

"Oh, and Dahlia?" He says, pausing to look at me.

I hate that my name sounds different coming from his mouth.

"Yes?" I ask, dread pooling in my stomach. I eye the handful of customers still browsing around the store. None of them seem to be paying attention, but I'm still hyper aware that we aren't alone.

I rush closer to him, so that we're standing face to face. "What is it?"

"It wouldn't be wise of you to ignore me again."

My stomach drops. "I didn't—"

"I know where you live, Bambi." His voice is casual, conversational. "And who you live with. I know where you get your coffee every morning." He says, his smile sharp. "And I know you've been smelling my jacket every night instead of throwing it away like you should have."

My blood runs cold. "You've been watching me."

"Every day." He confirms. "You said we were friends. Friends check in."

"That's not friendship." I hiss. "That's stalking."

"Tomato, tomahto." He shrugs, completely unbothered. "Answer my text next time."

"And if I don't?"

He looks at me, and something dark and hungry moves through his expression. It makes my breath catch for an entirely different reason than it should.

"If you don't..." He drawls. "Then, I'll have to get creative about getting your attention."

He smiles at me, seemingly unfazed by the obvious threat he just threw at me. "See you soon, Bambi."

The door chimes as he leaves, and I'm left standing by the door with my heart pounding and my skin still tingling in all the places he touched me.

Echo was here for less than fifteen minutes, and somehow

this whole place feels like his now. Like he's marked it. Claimed it. Claimed *me*.

I pull out my phone and stare at our text thread. At the question I never answered. I ignored it, thinking he'd just forget about me, but I couldn't have been more wrong.

I look out the window, checking to make sure he's gone, and when I find him staring back at me, a lump forms in my throat.

He's sitting in a car parked across the street, with the windows down, keys tossed on the dash, and his eyes locked on me.

The asshole is literally stalking me in broad daylight and he isn't even trying to hide it.

I should call the police. I should do something. Instead, I stand there, with my fingers pressed against the glass, staring back at him.

And the worst part of all?

Some fucked up part of me actually likes that he's watching.

# CHAPTER SEVEN

DAHLIA

THE SCENT OF PAPERBACKS AND WARM VANILLA FILLS THE AIR as I reorganize the shelves in Better Than Fiction for what feels like the hundredth time tonight. The store looks pristine, with its warm lighting, cozy reading nooks, and tall shelves full of happily-ever-afters. Everything is perfect. *Peaceful.* And still, I feel on edge.

Maybe it's leftover adrenaline from seeing Echo in my space yesterday, or maybe it's just my brain's way of telling me I've been alone with my thoughts for too long. Either way, with only twenty minutes left until we close, I'm ready for this day to be over.

My phone buzzes in my pocket, and when I pull it out and see Echo's name flashing on the screen, I drop the damn thing like it burned me.

It clatters against the ground, and I just stare at it for a second, waiting for it to attack me.

*Get it together.*

*You're fine.*

I pick up my phone and flip it face down on the coffee table without reading the message.

I tell myself it's because I don't owe him anything. That yesterday was a onetime, deeply fucked-up encounter that ended the moment he walked out of the shop. But then my phone buzzes again, and dread sinks deep into my gut.

*Shit. He warned me what would happen if I ignored him. Do I really want to give him a reason to come here?*

I exhale through my nose and slowly turn it over.

> Echo: You're avoiding me again.

> Echo: See.

*Fuck.*

I didn't think he'd notice.

A hollow laugh bubbles out of me before I can stop it.

*Of course* he noticed.

He's arrogant, presumptuous, and far too perceptive.

Now that he's reached out again, ignoring him feels like the wrong move.

He's already curious about me, and curiosity turns into persistence if I'm not careful. I need to do what I always do when people get too close. Push, deflect, and stay sharp enough to keep distance, but funny enough to make it seem accidental. Eventually, he'll tire of my attitude and move on.

I type out a response, my fingers stiff over the screen.

> Am I? Or have I just been too busy with work to respond to the egomaniac who strong-armed his way into my contacts?

I stare at the message, jaw tight, with my thumb hovering over the send button. It's sharp and a little defensive, but it works.

Before I can overthink it, I hit send.

> You're the one who wanted to be friends
> with me, Bambi.

I press my lips together. I don't like that he has a nick-name for me. It suggests a sense of familiarity that we don't have.

> True.

> But I was desperate.

I pause, then add,

> So really, this friendship was kind of a last
> resort.

There's a pause. Not a long one, but enough to make me wonder if I took it too far.

> So we are friends.

I exhale and lean my hip against the counter.

> Unfortunately

> How are you?

> Fine, I guess. My face still looks like I lost a
> fight with a brick wall.

> It looked bad yesterday.

> Wow. Thanks for the compliment

There's a pause. Longer this time. I'm halfway to setting my phone down when it buzzes again.

What's your favorite way to spend a day off?

Alone

Not out with friends?

I like quiet

Noted.

I'm debating on how to respond when my phone buzzes with an incoming call.

It's Josh.

My stomach flips and I silence it immediately, waiting until it goes to voicemail. A text from him comes through seconds later.

Can we talk? I miss you.

I clear the notification without responding and go back to Echo's message. I'm not ready to open that can of worms back up. Not tonight. Maybe not ever.

Echo's next text comes through.

What did you want to be when you grew up?

I blink. *That's… oddly specific.*

My thumbs hover.

I should just lie. It's what I usually do when anyone asks something real. But maybe the truth is better. Maybe the ugliness of it will get him to see he doesn't want someone like me in his life.

I wanted to be a mom.

A pause.

Do you still want that?

I swallow.

It's not really in the cards for me anymore.

Three dots. Gone, then back.

Sorry.

Wow. You should write sympathy cards.

I mean it. You seem like you'd be a good mother.

You don't even know me.

You stepped in for a stranger, knowing you couldn't win. I know enough.

The questions from him continue after that. Some are easy. Others aren't. I answer a few without thinking. Dodge the rest before he can push for more.

Are you always this inquisitive?

Only when I'm taking something seriously.

Ready for the next one?

Do you have a list or something?

There's a pause. A real one this time. Longer than before.

No.

There's definitely a fucking list.

You hesitated.

You're very observant.

You're very bad at lying.

I don't usually need to.

That, I believe.

My turn to ask a question?

Sure.

What did you want to be when you grew up?

There's no pause this time.

Someone who kept people safe.

I start to type out a response, but another text comes in almost immediately.

I'll save the rest of my questions for another
time.

Why?

It's late. I'm sure you've got things to wrap
up at work.

I glance at the clock. 9:15 p.m. I should've closed up shop a while ago.

Right.

Goodnight, Bambi. We'll continue this
tomorrow.

Not talk. *Continue.* Like this is something that will be ongoing. *Fucking hell.*

I lock the screen and tuck my phone back into my pocket, feeling like I gave him more than I meant to and kind of hating myself for it.

# CHAPTER EIGHT

*Echo*

THE INTERIOR OF MY AUDI RS7 IS DARK, SAVE FOR THE PALE light of my phone screen reflecting faintly off my windshield. The street is quiet, and the only sound I hear is the soft ticking of my engine as it cools.

I scroll through the text thread. Stop. Then scroll again. Same result.

The questions are fine. Neutral. Designed to invite elaboration without pressure.

*What's your favorite way to spend a day off?*

*What did you want to be when you were younger?*

*What do you value most?*

She answered every one of them, and still gave me nothing.

No emotional hooks. No leverage. Not even a pattern I could trace with any kind of certainty. Every response was a closed door disguised as politeness.

Most people need to be understood. They fill the silence when you give them space, and mistake undivided attention for safety. She didn't, and that's a problem.

I lock the screen and toss the phone aside, my jaw tight enough to ache.

Across from me, Better Than Fiction is still open, its lit front windows softening the edges of the otherwise dark city street. Every other storefront on the street is closed, only hers is open.

I don't like that.

From here, I can see her clearly enough to follow the rhythm of her movements. The way she leans over the shelves as she dusts them. The way her shoulders stay tense even when nothing notable is happening.

I settle deeper into the driver's seat, adjusting just enough to keep her in view without drawing attention. Anyone passing by would assume I belong here.

Bambi doesn't know I'm watching her.

I should feel guilty about that, but I don't. She gave me an open invitation into her world; it isn't my fault for accepting it.

Movement on the sidewalk pulls my attention away from the window. A man has stopped three storefronts down from hers. He's average height, lean, and his hood is pulled up despite the weather being mild enough not to warrant it. He stands there with his hands in his pockets, peering through the dark window. My gaze tracks him automatically.

He moves on after a moment and stops at the next window. Leans against the glass and looks longer than necessary. Then the next.

The street is quiet enough that I can hear the soft scuff of his shoes against the pavement. I straighten slightly in my seat.

This time he pauses directly across from Better Than Fiction, close enough that the light from the windows brushes his face. I can't see his expression clearly, but I can tell his attention is fixed on the inside of the store.

On *her*.

Annoyance settles low in my chest. Her shop shouldn't be the only one open this late. It's careless. An invitation for trouble she doesn't even realize she's extending.

The man glances down the empty street, then back at her windows, and starts crossing the street. I get out of the car and follow. I don't rush or announce myself, and when I stop beside him, he startles.

"They're closed," I say mildly, following his line of sight to the storefront. "Everything on this block is."

His eyes flick to me. Narrow and assessing. "I was just looking."

"Don't," I reply.

He shifts his weight, shoulders tensing. "Didn't realize that was illegal."

"It doesn't need to be."

Up close, he smells wrong. Stale and nervous.

"Why are you still here?"

His weak jaw tightens. "I'm leaving."

"Good." I step closer, just enough to make my point land. "Do that."

He hesitates, and my patience wears thin.

I grab him by the collar of his sweatshirt and lift him off the ground.

"Listen carefully," I say quietly. "You don't come back to this street. You don't look into these stores. You don't even think about the woman inside that shop."

His eyes widen, like he wasn't expecting me to know.

"And if I see you anywhere near here again—" I lean in close enough that he can feel the heat of my breath. "I won't just make you disappear. I'll leave your body so unrecogniz-able, no one will be able to identify it. Do you understand?"

He nods frantically.

I lower him to his feet and pat his shoulder hard enough to make him stumble. "Good. Now get the fuck out of here."

He turns and jogs away, disappearing around the corner of the block without looking back.

I wait until I'm sure he's gone, then I return to my car.

I'm not sure how much time passes as I continue to watch her move around the bookstore. The rhythm of it settles in. She dusts, pauses, adjusts, pauses again. Until the details blur together.

Before I even realize she's finished, the last set of lights are flickering off and she's stepping outside into the night.

She locks the door behind her, and when she turns around and her gaze lifts, her eyes land straight on me.

My body reacts before my brain has the decency to catch up. I duck down instinctively, despite the tint being dark enough to hide me, and my foot slams on the brake before I can stop it.

*Shit.*

Her attention snaps to the red glow of the taillights, and her eyes narrow.

I turn the engine over, its roar loud on the quiet street, and slam my foot against the accelerator.

The car jumps forward, and the tires screech against the asphalt as I pull away from the curb and floor-it past her.

In the rearview, I catch her standing there, watching me leave with her keys clenched in her hand and her head tilted slightly.

I planned on following her home to make sure she got home safe, but being seen changes the equation. I need her comfortable, not paranoid.

I pull up the tracker I installed on her car earlier today, the one I slipped under her rear bumper while she was opening the store, and track the blue dot as it starts moving toward her apartment.

*There.*

Problem solved.

I have other things to handle tonight anyway. Things that actually matter. Things that don't revolve around an evasive brunette with a propensity for danger.

# CHAPTER NINE

GETTING TO KNOW BAMBI BETTER HAS PROVEN TO BE QUITE the challenge.

I've spent the last couple of weeks digging up everything I could on her. But every time I get close to a trace of information, I hit a wall. No school or medical records. No personal social media. Not even a fucking digital trail.

I was only able to find her bookstore because her cell number is tied to its social media account. And even that's curated. There are no photos of her on it. No tags. No trace of the woman at all.

So I got creative.

Installing spyware on her phone wasn't hard. We have a former NSA agent on our payroll who builds custom surveillance packages for us. Once he threw it together, all it took was disguising the link as a small picture of my childhood pet, so she'd have no reason not to click it.

Now I can see everything. Her location. Her messages. Her calls. And tonight, when she gets home, I'll watch her sleep from the camera on her computer. The one she doesn't know I have access to.

For the last week, I've been watching her. All day. Every day. Between meetings. Between calls. Every spare moment I have has been consumed by her.

Is that extreme?

*Probably.*

She wanted to be friends, and this is my kind of friendship.

I take a seat at my desk and pull up the security feeds at Better Than Fiction.

She's wearing that black turtleneck again. The same one from last week. The one that hugs her curves and makes me think about peeling it off her while she trembles underneath me.

It's supposed to hide the marks on her neck. The ones those assholes left when they tried to choke her. But all it does is make me want to put new ones there. Ones that she'll enjoy. Ones that show she's mine.

She has no idea how close I came to losing my control that day. She let me touch her skin, let me feel her pulse racing under my fingertips, and she let me look deeply into those beautiful brown eyes of hers.

She wanted me to kiss her.

I could see it. I could feel it in my fucking chest. And I've been thinking about her mouth ever since.

———

BAMBI IS IN THE BOOKSTORE PAST 9PM AGAIN.

She's the only light on the entire block. Every other business closed hours ago, leaving her alone in a pool of yellow light that might as well be a fucking beacon.

She doesn't see the man across the street. The one who's been standing there for the last eight minutes, watching her through the window. But I do.

My hand tightens around my phone.

This is the third time this week. Different men. Same pattern. They drift past. They linger. They watch. And she has no idea.

*Who the hell opens a bookshop near a known drug area?*
Bambi.

That's who.

I shoot off a text to one of our men nearby before I rip my fucking hair out.

Three minutes later, he shows up and parks himself across the street from her store. His orders are clear. Stay unseen, only intervene if absolutely necessary. Bambi's still inside restocking shelves, blissfully unaware of the lengths I have to go through to keep her safe.

I make a call to her property manager next. The conversation lasts about two minutes and after a little smooth talking and a heavy donation routed through the right shell, starting tomorrow businesses on Bambi's block will close at seven.

This isn't about control, it's about correction. She stays open too late. She's alone too often. Someone has to compensate for that.

I lean back in my chair and stare at the ceiling of my office.

*When the hell did this become my new normal?*

I haven't slept well in days. Not since I realized being her friend was more complicated than I initially thought. She's just so reckless.

Friends shouldn't have to change your business's operating hours. Friends shouldn't have to worry about how long you stay out after dark. Friends shouldn't have to access your street's surveillance feeds to make sure you're safe.

I pull up a new window on the screen and scan through her call logs, just to see if there's anything new.

One name keeps resurfacing.

*Josh.*

Four calls this week. A handful of texts. None of them answered.

*Good.*

She doesn't want him. I can see it in the way she silences his calls. The way she deletes his voicemails without bothering to listen to them.

She wants me.

She texts me back every single time. Even when she's telling me to fuck off, she's engaging. She could block my number. Report me. Hell, even call the cops, but she doesn't. Because some part of her likes this. Likes that I'm paying attention. Likes that I'm always there.

I pull up the store's feed again to check on her. She's moved closer to the front window now and is organizing the books in the display. Her long, dark hair is tied back today, and as she bends over to pick something up, a strand falls into her face. My hands itch with the urge to touch it.

She's become an addiction. An obsession. And the longer I watch, the harder it is to look away.

"Hey, creeper." Athena laughs, sneaking up behind me.

I slam my laptop shut and glare at her. "Jesus Athena, ever heard of knocking?"

"Where's the fun in that?" She asks, rounding my desk as her eyes dance with mischief.

"So…" She singsongs. "Who's the girl you're stalking?"

I frown. "No one, and I'm not stalking anyone."

"Right." She hops up on my desk, completely unbothered by my death stare.

"Well, that 'no one' sure is pretty."

I scowl at her. "What do you want, Athena?"

"In-N-Out. River's busy." She shrugs. "I need human interaction."

"Take security."

She rolls her eyes. "I want a conversation, not a shadow."

"Take Briggs."

The shift in her expression is instant. Her smile falters just slightly before she schools her features back to neutral.

"He wouldn't want to go with me." She mutters.

"Did you ask him?"

"Whatever." She slides off my desk, suddenly eager to leave. "I'll figure it out."

She pauses at the door and looks back at me. "You should get out of this office. You're acting weird."

"That's what you always say."

"Yeah." Her eyes soften slightly. "But this feels different."

The door shuts behind her, and I'm left wondering what the hell she meant by that.

---

I step out onto the balcony to get some air and find River standing near the railing with his phone pressed to his ear and tension radiating through every muscle in his body.

He's in his element. Managing crisis. Calculating angles. Controlling variables. He was born for this. The politics. The strategy. The restraint.

He's just finishing the call as I approach.

"Casello?" I ask.

He nods, scrubbing a hand over his face. "I just got word from one of our allies that he's been asking around for footage of that night. Apparently, cell towers put his men within a half-mile radius of Oracle. He doesn't have proof yet, but his suspicion is growing."

"Let it." I say with a shrug. "He won't find anything."

"Briggs is double-checking surveillance, anyway. Bars, ATMs, anything that might've caught movement in the area." River turns to face me fully. "You're sure no one saw what happened?"

"I already told you, I'm sure."

He studies me for a moment, and I wonder if he can see through me the way Athena can. If he can tell I'm lying.

"Sorry to keep asking you." He says, his voice quiet. "I'm just worried about what'll happen if it comes out."

"If it does, I'll handle it."

River shakes his head. "No. You've always taken on the brunt of things. Even when you didn't deserve to. Especially then." He pauses, his eyes flicking to mine as a flicker of shame crosses his face. "If shit hits the fan, promise me you won't try to handle it alone. "

I clench my jaw, hating how real the conversation turned. "Okay." I mutter. "I promise."

"Good." He says, clapping a hand on my shoulder before heading back inside. "And get some sleep. You look like shit."

I give him a nod and stare out at the grounds surrounding our family home. It's an imposing place. All stone and iron and calculated intimidation. My father purposely designed it that way. For it to be a physical representation of the power he held, not only over this city, but over everyone in his home. I spent most of my childhood wishing I could burn it to the ground. Then my father died, and everything that made this place unbearable went with him. The memories of his cruelty are still here, embedded into the walls and into the recesses of my mind. But so are the people worth staying for.

A few weeks ago, Bambi was a stranger. A loose end that turned into something else entirely. I can tell myself that I'm not doing anything wrong. That I'm able to handle my obligations to this family while also keeping her in my life.

But when I return to my office and take a seat back at my desk, one thought keeps circling my mind. River isn't an idiot, and sooner or later, he's going to find out about Bambi's involvement. When he does, he'll want me to take care of the problem. The logical choice is obvious. River is my brother. My family. The person I've bled for more times than I can count. Bambi is... something else.

The choice should be easy.

So why does the thought of putting a bullet through her skull make me want to gouge my own eyes out?

# CHAPTER TEN

DAHLIA

IT'S BEEN OVER TWO WEEKS SINCE ECHO SHOWED UP AT MY bookstore, and in that time, he's texted me every day.

Not just once, either. Multiple times. Morning check-ins, random observations, questions that feel designed to map the inside of my head.

*What are you afraid of?*

*What do you regret?*

*What do you want that you won't let yourself have?*

I answer some. Deflect others. But I always respond. Because the alternative is him showing up in person again, and after what went down last time, I'm not sure I can handle that.

The memory of that day is singed in my brain. The feel of his fingers on my neck, of his thumb pressed against my pulse, and of the way he looked at me like he wanted to devour me whole. All of it haunts me.

I've probably replayed that moment in my head at least a hundred times. Which is pathetic. And dangerous. And exactly the kind of thinking that's going to get me killed.

My phone buzzes on the nightstand with an incoming text from Echo.

What are you doing?

I glance at the clock. 9:43 PM.

About to go to bed. Why?

Liar. You haven't even changed into your pajamas yet.

My stomach drops and I scan my room, expecting to find him standing in a corner somewhere with that infuriating smirk.

He does this all the time. Casually mentions things he shouldn't know about. Like what I'm wearing. Or that I took a different route to work. Or that I skipped lunch.

I still don't know how he does it. I've checked the apartment for cameras and my car for trackers dozens of times, and still nothing.

Lately I've been telling myself that he has some kind of stalker sixth sense, just so I can sleep better at night.

It's absolutely fucked up. But here we are.

Stalker

Admirer.

I hate that it makes me smile.

---

I'M LYING IN MY BED, FRESHLY SHOWERED, SCROLLING ON MY phone when an article comes across my newsfeed.

Top Ten Teenage Killers.

Against my better judgement, I click on it.

It doesn't take me long to find the profile on Christian. He's ranked number 8 on the list. The fact that they're even ranking monsters like him is disgusting.

I try to skim through it, but my eyes keep catching on all the horrific details, and I can't stop picturing my parents in my head.

How scary it must've been for them. How painful. How awful it must've been for my dad to have to watch my mom die, and to know he wouldn't be able to protect me.

I keep reading through blurry eyes, and *God,* I hate how they're sensationalizing that night. How they're focusing their lens on Christian's violence and his twisted psyche, as if he's something to be in awe of.

It was a fucking tragedy. The most tragic night of my life, but aside from their names, they're barely acknowledging my parents at all. There's no mention of how loved they were or how impactful their loss was. No mention of who they were as individuals or the loving friends and family they left behind. They're only focusing on their death and how violent it was. As if their death serves as nothing more than a form of entertainment.

The sound of metal sliding against metal sounds from somewhere behind me. My head snaps up and I freeze.

The sliding glass door. Someone's opening the sliding glass door. How is that even possible? We're on the fourth floor.

I scramble to my feet just in time to see Echo stepping into my room.

"What the hell are you doing here?" I ask, my voice shaking.

"Checking on you." He says, stepping closer. His eyes

sweep over me, cataloguing everything. His jaw tightens. "What's wrong?"

"Nothing." I say, shaking my head dismissively.

"You're crying."

"No, I'm not—" I snap, pressing my fingers to my face automatically. They come back wet.

*Fuck.*

I am, and I didn't even realize it.

I narrow my eyes at him. "That doesn't matter. You can't be here."

"But I am." He says, taking a step closer. "Now, tell me what happened."

"I already told you it's nothing." I say, gritting my teeth. "Now go." I move towards him and press my hands against his chest to try to push him back toward the patio door.

He doesn't move an inch.

It's like pushing against a wall of solid muscle. Heat radiates through his shirt, and I can feel his heart beating steady and strong beneath my palms.

I shove harder, and he just stands there, watching me with those intense amber eyes.

"Give me a name." He says quietly, his voice dropping to something more cold and dangerous. "That's all I need."

"There is no name." I say, pushing again as frustrated tears burn my eyes. "Just get out!"

"No."

"Echo stop—"

"Someone hurt you. Tell me who."

I look up at him, ready to scream, ready to shove him again, and the words die in my throat.

He's looking at me with the same intensity he did in the bookstore. Like he's been starving for weeks and I'm the only thing that will satisfy his hunger.

I should be thinking about my past. I should be dwelling on my guilt and all my mistakes. But with Echo here, standing this close, and looking at me like that, he's all I can focus on. And a twisted part of me is fiending for a distraction.

I take in everything. From the way his lips are slightly parted, to the way his throat keeps bobbing up and down.

I need to step back. To put distance between us before things go any further. But my legs still aren't moving.

I swallow hard and look up at him as my hands press against the hard planes of his chest and I feel the steady rhythm of his heart beating.

"Stop looking at me like that, Bambi."

"Why?" I ask, my voice barely above a whisper.

"Because you won't like what happens next."

I lick my lips and stare at him even harder, extending a clear challenge with my eyes.

His pupils dilate, and my pulse is racing so fast I can hear it in my ears.

*This is so fucked up. This is reckless. This is—*

I don't get to finish the thought before he's on me.

His mouth crashes into mine and every other thought in my head flies out the window. All I can think about is him. His scent. His warmth. His tongue.

His lips are soft yet demanding as they move against mine with a feral intensity that is as sexy as it is terrifying. His velvety tongue slides against mine, and I moan into his mouth at the sensation.

*Jesus, Mary, and Joseph, his tongue has no business feeling this good.*

Echo hoists me up by my thighs, and I wrap my legs around his waist as he walks us backwards towards the bed. He sits on the edge, and I settle on top of his lap, straddling him as our mouths move in tangent with each other.

Echo bucks his hips and suddenly, I'm hyperaware of the feel of him underneath me. He's hard, thick, and pressed firmly against the seam of my pussy. The sensation is so delicious, so goddamn overwhelming, that I can't help but grind against him as I whimper into his mouth.

"Jesus Christ, Bambi." He rasps, breaking our kiss. "You're going to kill me."

"Good." I breathe, grinding against him even harder. "Consider it payback for the night we met."

I go in for another kiss and when our tongues touch, Echo groans into my mouth.

The sound reverberates straight to my pussy.

*Fuck.*

How is he so hot?

Echo smiles against my mouth. "Genetics, mostly."

I blink a few times before it clicks.

I said that out loud.

*Oh my god.*

I said that out loud.

I feel the heat of embarrassment rising up my neck, but before it can fully hit, Echo distracts me by sliding his hands down to my ass and gripping it tightly, helping me chase the delicious friction.

"You have no idea what the fuck you do to me, Bambi." He breathes.

He squeezes harder, the sensation hitting the point where pleasure and pain beautifully collide, and my eyes roll back.

*Fuck.*

Heat pools between my legs. I swirl my hips on top of him and I can feel myself soaking through my thin sleep shorts.

I know Echo feels it too because as I keep grinding his breathing gets more and more ragged.

"Dahlia—" He sighs, my name sounding like a prayer, a plea, and a warning all wrapped in one.

I don't stop. I couldn't even if I wanted to. All I can think about is the way his cock feels beneath me. The way his hands feel so perfect on my skin. The way his mouth tastes like mint and a hint of smoke.

Keeping one palm firmly on my ass, he slides his other hand higher and palms my breast over my thin robe. His thumb brushes against my nipple and my whole body trembles.

"Fuck," he says, pulling back to look me in my eyes. "You like that don't you, Bambi?"

I sink my teeth into my lower lip and nod, not even caring how crazy this is.

I'm lost in it. Lost in him and in the way his touch makes everything else in the world disappear. My past doesn't exist. My guilt doesn't exist. There's only this. Him. Me. Us.

He pinches my nipple hard as he pulls me in for another deep kiss, and I groan into his mouth.

*How is he so good at this?*

His mouth moves to my neck, sucking and biting in a way that's definitely going to leave marks, and I don't even care. I just tilt my head back to give him better access and grind myself against cock even harder.

Echo bucks his hips, slamming his thick, rigid cock right against my clit until my whole body starts to tremble.

I'm so close to coming.

So close to completely shattering all over him.

Then the sound of the front door slamming snaps both of us out of our trance.

Fallon's home.

*Shit. Shit. Shit.*

I shove myself away from Echo's chest and he lets go of me immediately.

"You need to leave." I hiss, trying to catch my breath. "Now."

He touches his swollen lips, and something dark and possessive flashes across his face.

"Make it worth my while."

I glare at him incredulously. "What?"

His eyes drop to my chest. To my hardened nipples visible through my thin robe. He licks his lips.

*Oh.*

"You're insane." I whisper.

"And you're wasting time." He says, leaning back on my bed. "Unless you want me to call her in here?"

"You wouldn't." I challenge.

"I might."

I glare at him as I debate reaching for the tie on my robe.

*Whatever,* it's not like he wasn't just touching them a second ago. Besides, I'd be lying if I said a part of me isn't a little curious about what his reaction will be.

Before I can talk myself out of it, I grab the edges of my robe and flash him before closing it again.

Echo's smile is absolutely sinful and I bite the inside of my cheek to stop from smiling back at him.

"There." I hiss, narrowing my eyes at him. "Happy?"

"Very." He says smoothly as he stands and backs himself towards the patio door.

"You have gorgeous tits, Bambi." He sinks his teeth into his bottom lip. "I can't wait to get my teeth on them."

My face flames, and I nearly choke on my own saliva. "That is not happening."

"We'll see about that." He says, stepping out onto the patio, looking way too satisfied with himself.

"Oh, and Bambi…" He says, pausing just before he slides the door shut. "Make sure to lock this after I leave."

Then he's gone, disappearing into the night like he was never there.

I lock the sliding door with shaking hands and press my back against the cool glass.

I read an article about my psycho ex and the first thing I do is dry-hump a killer. The same killer who's been openly stalking me for the last month.

*What the hell is wrong with me?*

# CHAPTER ELEVEN

Echo

I MAKE IT ABOUT THREE BLOCKS DOWN FROM HER APARTMENT building before I have to pull over. The engine ticks as I sit in the dark with my hands still wrapped tightly around the steering wheel.

I tried to focus on the road, but I can't even think straight right now. All I can think about is her. I can still taste her on my lips, and the smell of her skin is everywhere. In my nose. In my head. In my fucking veins. Even my poor cock is suffering. The fucker is still hard as a rock.

I squeeze the steering wheel until my knuckles turn white. *Fuck.*

I shouldn't have left. I should've ignored the interruption and told her to keep grinding on my dick. Should've let her dry-fuck me to the point where her primal need outweighed her logic, and she begged me to fuck her. But I needed to get the hell out of that building.

It's not like I suddenly grew a conscience. I don't have one, and even if I did, there's no line I wouldn't cross for her.

I left because I knew that once I got a taste of that sweet

little cunt of hers, there would be no going back to pretending we're just friends. And Bambi isn't ready for what happens when we stop pretending. Not yet, anyway.

I pull out my phone and navigate to the app that accesses the camera in her room. The feed loads and shows her empty bedroom. She's probably out in the living room with her roommate, an area I still don't have access to.

I should drive home, get some sleep, and give her space to process what happened. A normal man would. Instead, I recline my seat, settle in, and wait. Because I already know I'm not going anywhere until I see her again.

Six minutes later, Bambi's door opens, and she slips inside before gently closing it behind her. She stands there for a minute, pressed against the door, staring at her bed as her chest rises and falls in rapid succession.

*Is she thinking about me?*

Her hand drifts to her mouth, fingers ghosting over lips that are still swollen from my kiss. Then lower, to her neck where I bit and sucked hard enough to leave marks. She closes her eyes and her thighs press tightly together.

*Good girl.*

*You should be thinking about me.*

She pushes off the door and moves to her bed, climbing under the covers fully clothed. She thinks she's going to sleep. That she can just ignore the arousal still thrumming through her body, if she tries hard enough.

*Adorable.* She doesn't realize I've already ruined sleeping in that bed for her. And in all fairness, she ruined sleep for me weeks ago.

I've never had someone get under my skin like this. Not in a way that makes me rearrange my entire day just to watch her organize paperbacks. Not in a way that makes me check my phone every thirty seconds just to see if she replied.

I kill people for a living, for God's sakes. My brother and I have maintained our family's empire with violence and fear, and calculated cruelty. And somehow, this girl. This interesting, impulsive, infuriating girl has me sitting in my car at 10:30 at night, hard as fuck, desperate to see her face.

On screen, Bambi tosses restlessly. The covers twist around her legs as she shifts from her back to her side, then back again.

She's trying to fight it. I can see it in every frustrated movement. But her body won't let her forget me.

After five minutes of watching her fail to settle, she throws the covers off with a frustrated groan, most likely directed at me. She sits up, runs her hands through her hair, and stares at the ceiling like she's searching for strength. Then her hand moves to her nightstand.

My breath hitches as she pulls open the drawer and retrieves a small purple vibrator.

*Oh, Bambi.*

My cock, which had finally relaxed, goes rock hard in an instant.

This is crossing a line. Not a moral one. I crossed that weeks ago when I started watching her. But this is different. This is intimate in a way that should make me close the feed and drive away. But *goddamnit,* I can't look away even if I wanted to.

I should have boundaries with her. Lines that I won't cross even in the depths of my obsession. But every rule I've ever had dissolves the moment she's involved.

Don't make things personal? Failed that one in the alley. Don't create any liabilities? She's been one since the night I let her live. Don't mix business with pleasure? I'm watching the witness I should've killed through an illegally hacked camera. And now this.

*Don't watch her touch herself, you sick fuck.*

Even as the thought forms, I'm already unzipping my jeans. My hand wraps around my cock and I hiss at the contact. I'm so fucking hard it hurts.

On screen, she's sliding her shorts down her legs, and even through the grainy feed I can see how wet her panties are.

*She's soaked.*

Because of me. Because of what we did on that bed. The knowledge sends a shiver of satisfaction through me.

She positions herself against her pillows, legs spreading, and for a moment she just breathes.

*Fuck.*

*She's trying to talk herself out of this.*

*Don't.* I think, stroking my cock. *Don't you dare fucking stop.*

Her hand moves between her legs, touching herself over her underwear first, testing. Her hips jerk at the contact, and I stroke myself harder.

I've imagined this. Late at night, when I should be sleeping, I've pictured her exactly like this. Desperate and needy and thinking about me.

But imagination has nothing on reality. Nothing on watching her slide her underwear to the side and seeing how wet she actually is for me. Nothing on watching her turn on the vibrator and immediately press it between her legs with a gasp.

She reaches for her pillow, pressing it to her face.

*Smart girl.*

Can't let your roommate hear what I do to you. Can't let anyone know you're touching yourself while thinking about the man you should be keeping at arm's length.

Her hips start rolling and I match her rhythm, stroking

myself in time with her movements. I imagine it's my hand between her legs. My mouth. My cock buried deep inside her while she screams my name.

On screen, her movements become more frantic. Her back arches harder. Her free hand fists the sheets.

*She's close.*

I can tell by the way her whole body tenses, by the way her hips chase the vibrator with increasing desperation.

My hand moves faster, my own orgasm building at the base of my spine.

Then her mouth moves against the pillow. And I read my name on her lips.

*Echo.*

She's silently moaning my fucking name. Coming to the thought of *me*. The knowledge destroys me.

My vision whites out as my orgasm hits with enough force to leave me shuddering. I come harder than I have in years. Her name, a broken curse in the silence of my car as I paint my hand and steering wheel with the evidence of how fucked I am.

When I can finally breathe again, my vision clears and I look back at the screen to find her lying there, just as shaken as I am. She looks as satisfied as she is unsettled, which is profoundly amusing to me. I smile to myself as I tuck my cock back into my jeans and clean myself up.

Bambi gave me something tonight that she had no intention of giving me. Proof that I'm not the only one losing control.

This isn't one-sided anymore.

This is mutual destruction.

And it's time for Bambi to come to the same conclusion I have. We are inevitable.

# CHAPTER TWELVE

DAHLIA

I'M STANDING IN THE PASTA AISLE HOLDING A PLASTIC BASKET full of things I don't remember choosing, wondering how I ended up here.

Not the grocery store. I know how that happened. Fallon strong-armed me into leaving the apartment with promises of snacks and sunlight, like I'm a feral cat she's trying to rehabilitate.

*No.*

I'm wondering how I ended up involved with someone like Echo.

Less than twenty-four hours ago, I was straddling Echo in my bedroom. Grinding against him like I was trying to fuse our bodies together. Moaning into his mouth while his hands gripped my ass.

And then, as if that wasn't bad enough, I flashed him. I pulled my robe open and showed him my tits just because he asked me to. Not to mention what I did after he left.

*What the hell is wrong with me?*

I squeeze my eyes shut and press my fingers against

my temples. This is exactly why I let Fallon drag me to the grocery store. I need normal and mundane. I need to pick a pasta and make dinner and pretend like I didn't almost come on my stalker's lap less than twelve hours ago.

I shift the basket on my arm and stare at the shelves in front of me without really seeing them. There are too many options, and my brain is too frazzled to commit to any of them. With the thoughts of what happened with Echo constantly circling, I don't have the bandwidth to think about anything else.

Fallon disappeared down the frozen foods aisle a minute ago with a dramatic announcement about fiending for some ice cream, but I didn't go with her. I needed to be alone and just think for a little while.

My phone buzzes with an incoming text from Echo.

What are you up to?

I shouldn't respond, but I do anyway.

Shopping, why?

The response comes immediately.

Not sure if I'd consider staring at the same shelf for two minutes shopping. Tell me, Bambi, are you thinking about me?

My eyes snap up, scanning the aisle frantically. He isn't anywhere in sight. There's just a woman comparing sauce jars and an elderly man reaching for a box of linguine.

Are you in here somewhere?

> Answer my question first, then I'll answer
> yours.

> I'm not thinking about anything. I was just
> dazing off.

> That's a shame. Because I've been thinking
> about you. About how you tasted and how
> you sounded when you whimpered my
> name. How wet you were when you—

I lock the screen and shove my phone so hard into my pocket that I almost drop my basket. My face is on fire. And heat is already pooling between my thighs.

*This is bad.*

*This is so fucking bad.*

I'm halfway through a mental argument with myself about whether I should leave when a familiar voice cuts through my thoughts.

"Dahlia?"

My spine stiffens.

I recognize that voice.

*Josh.*

I turn slowly, as if delaying the moment will somehow make it easier to deal with.

Josh stands at the end of the aisle, one hand tucked into the pocket of his jacket, the other holding a carton of almond milk. His smile is tentative and hopeful in a way that makes me feel awful.

"I thought I saw your car out there." He says, nodding vaguely toward the front of the store. "I wasn't sure if it was you."

*Of course* he noticed my car. I tighten my grip on the basket. "Yeah. I'm just here grabbing a few things."

He steps closer carefully, like he's afraid he might spook me. "You haven't been answering my calls." His voice doesn't sound accusatory. It just sounds… sad. Which makes me feel even worse.

I wince. "I know. I'm sorry."

"Did I do something?" He asks, and the genuine confusion in voice makes me want to scream.

No, Josh. You didn't do anything. You're perfectly nice and safe and everything I *should* want.

The problem is that a month ago I met this killer who won't leave me alone and yesterday I ended up dry-humping him so hard, I almost came all over him.

"No." I say honestly. "You didn't."

"Then why won't you talk to me?" He steps closer, and I can see him trying to puzzle me out. "I thought we had something good."

We had fine at best. Every kiss we ever shared was utterly forgettable. *Nothing like what I have with Echo.*

I catch the thought and mentally shove it away. I don't have anything with Echo. Just a weird sexual attraction I need to get out of my system.

"I've been thinking." I say carefully. "And I don't think it's fair to keep seeing you when I know this isn't going anywhere."

It's not the full truth, but it's the closest thing to it that won't make this completely awkward.

His face falls. "Because of what Nate said? Because I swear, I never called you—"

"It's not about that." I assure him, even though it's partially about that. "I just—I can't give you what you want."

His brow knits. "But all I want is you."

"No." I say, shaking my head. "You want someone who

can love you back. You deserve that. I can't. I won't. So it's better if we just—"

"Let me decide what's better for me." He says, cutting me off. There's an edge to his voice I've never heard before. "I'm a patient man, dollface. I'm willing to wait."

He reaches out for me instinctively, and when I feel his fingers close around my wrist, my world tilts.

His hold isn't hard or violent. It's barely even pressure. But my body doesn't care about that distinction. My chest tightens and my pulse roars in my ears as dark memories slams into me all at once.

*Hands holding me still. Hands deciding for me. Hands that wouldn't let go.*

"Josh stop—" I start, but my voice fractures, and his hands stay locked firmly around my wrist. He's saying something to me, but I can't hear anything beyond the pounding of my own heartbeat.

Then suddenly, Josh isn't touching me anymore.

He's gasping, his face contorted in pain as his arm is pried away and twisted behind his back at an angle that makes my stomach churn.

I look up.

Echo is here, standing right beside me, holding Josh's arm with what looks like minimal effort.

The look on his face is the same one he had in the alley. Cold. Lethal. And cruel. He looks like he's calculating exactly how much force it would take to break Josh's arm and deciding if it's worth the spectacle.

For a split second, my brain tries to latch onto the other version of him. The one from last night. The one from my phone who checks in on me and asks questions and makes my heart flutter.

Then I look at the expression on his face again, and a cold

feeling slithers down my spine. This isn't the man who was in my room last night. This is the one from the alley. The one who stood over four bodies without flinching. The one who raised his gun and smiled at me like it was some kind of game.

Texting him blurred that image. Softened the edges. Made him feel... *safer*. But this, this is the real him.

I tighten my grip on the basket, using it as an anchor.

Josh tries to pull away, but Echo's grip only tightens. "What the fuck, man?" He whines.

"She asked you to stop." Echo hisses, his voice cold and lethal. "She shouldn't have to ask twice."

There's something about Echo's tone that makes my blood run cold. If Josh doesn't stop, he won't walk out of this grocery store alive.

"Let him go." I hear myself say.

Echo's eyes flick to me, and for a second, I think he might not listen. Then, slowly, he releases Josh with a controlled precision that somehow feels more threatening than the violence he just displayed.

Echo's expression is calm as he steps back and adjusts his cuffs like nothing happened. He doesn't look like he just grabbed someone at all. He looks like he just dealt with a minor inconvenience.

Josh stumbles back, clutching his arm to his chest. "Are you fucking insane? You could've broken my arm, man."

Echo doesn't give him a response. Instead, he moves closer to me and wraps his arm protectively around my shoulders.

I can feel the heat radiating off of his body in waves. It's the same heat I felt yesterday when I was on top of him. When his hands were guiding my hips. When I was so close to coming, I could taste it.

*Stop.*

*Fuck, I need to stop thinking about that.*

"You should go." I tell Josh, barely recognizing the sound of my own voice.

Josh's eyes dart between us, disbelief hardening into something ugly.

"Are you serious right now?" Josh's voice cracks. "Is this why you've been avoiding me? Because of him?"

*Yes.* I think to myself. But being honest right now feels like I'd be throwing salt on the wound. Still, I need to say something.

"Yes." Echo answers for me.

My head whips toward him, but if he notices, he doesn't react.

"She's mine now." He continues, his eyes locked on Josh with an intensity that makes my skin prickle. "She has been from the moment we met. Whatever this was?" He says, gesturing dismissively between Josh and me. "Is over."

The air leaves my lungs. This isn't just him being protective. This is him marking his fucking territory.

Josh scoffs. "Unbelievable." His gaze cuts to me, and there's hurt there, but there's also a lot of anger. "Dahlia, are you not going to say anything?"

"I'm sorry." I mumble, shaking my head. "I promise I'll text you later and explain everything. But please, just go."

Josh hesitates, his fists curling as his eyes flick between Echo and me, then after a few tense seconds he turns to leave. The moment he's out of sight, I elbow Echo hard in the stomach and slide out from under his arm.

"Ouch." He says mildly. "What was that for?"

"What the hell is wrong with you?" I hiss, keeping my voice low. "You can't just show up here and do that."

"What? Stop him from touching you without permission?"

"I was handling it." I hiss.

Echo's brow furrows. "You were panicking." He says, his voice softening slightly. "I could see it on your face, Bambi. The second he grabbed you, you froze and started shutting down."

He's right, but there's no way I'm admitting that right now. "That doesn't give you the right to assault him in the middle of a grocery store."

"I didn't assault him. I removed him." He steps closer, and I instinctively step back. "There is a difference, Bambi."

"Is there?" I'm shaking now, adrenaline and anger and frustration coursing through me. "Because from where I'm standing, you just assaulted someone and claimed me like I'm some kind of property."

"You are mine." He says simply. "We both know it."

"Oh my god. You're insane, and we are not having this conversation here." I snap.

"Fine. Where would you like to have it? Your bedroom? Because I have very fond memories of that location."

My face burns. "Stop."

"Why? You started something yesterday, Bambi. Did you think I'd just forget about it?"

"I didn't start anything. You're the one that kissed me."

"And you kissed me back." He says, his voice low in my ear. He takes another step forward, backing me up against the shelves. "You climbed on my lap. You dry-fucked me until you soaked through those cute little shorts. And you moaned my fucking name like it was a prayer."

"Shut up." I whisper desperately, my eyes darting to make sure no one can hear us.

"You showed me your tits." His voice drops even lower, intimate and devastating. "Not because I forced you. But because you wanted me to see them. You wanted me to remember them."

"That's not—"

"And now you're standing here pretending yesterday didn't happen." He sinks his teeth into his bottom lip, and I swallow hard. "But I can see it in your eyes, Bambi. You're thinking about it too. About how good it felt. About how close you were. And I bet if I slipped my hand between your legs right now, it'd come out glistening."

*He's right.* And I really fucking hate that he is.

"You need to leave." I force out.

"Why? Afraid of what you'll do if I stay?"

*Yes.*

I'm about to tell him to go to hell when I notice movement on the other end of the aisle. It's Fallon. She's rounding the corner

*Fuck.*

"Get out of here." I hiss, trying to shove him away.

My fingers press against his stomach, which is disturbingly solid, and the maniac actually smiles at me, like he knows what I'm thinking.

"Bambi, if you wanted an excuse to touch me again, you could've just asked."

I let out of huff of frustration and yank my hands away. "You're ridiculous."

He flashes a smile as his eyes gaze at something behind me. "And we have company."

I turn around to find Fallon standing in front of us with a pint of Ben & Jerry's in her hand and suspicion written all over her face.

Her gaze lands on Echo and sharpens immediately. I

watch her take in his expensive suit, his good looks, and the way he's still standing way too close to me.

"Dahlia…" she says softly, keeping her eyes locked on him. "Who is this?"

I open my mouth, but my brain has completely short-circuits.

Echo steps forward and extends his hand like some kind of gentleman. "I'm Echo," he says smoothly. "You must be Fallon. I've heard so much about you."

*When?* I want to scream. *When have you heard about her?*

Fallon hesitates, her eyes flicking to me for confirmation. When I don't immediately object, she slowly shakes his hand.

"Funny." She says, her grip lingering just long enough to make it pointed. "Because she's never mentioned you."

Echo's mouth twitches.

*Shit. Echo's unpredictable, and who knows what the hell will come out of his mouth.*

"I did." I blurt, jumping in before he can say anything else. "He's the guy who helped me the night I was mugged."

"Oh." Fallon says, her posture relaxing a fraction. "That was you?"

Echo glances at me, and there's clear amusement in his eyes. "Yeah. I suppose it was."

"Well, thank you for that." Fallon says, wrapping an arm around my shoulders to not so subtly pull me away from him. "There are way too many assholes in this world. It's good to know there's at least one good guy out there."

*Good.*

If only she knew.

"Well, it was nice seeing you again." I say, flashing Echo a polite smile. "Fal, you ready to go?"

Fallon eyes me for a second, then nods. "Yeah… sure."

"Why don't I walk you two out?" Echo offers. Before I can say anything to refuse, he reaches out and grabs both of our grocery baskets.

"Oh, you really don't have to—" I start.

"It's no problem." He replies, already walking towards the checkout. "Besides, I'd love to get to know Fallon better. Any friend of Bambi's is a friend of mine."

*Don't call me that in front of her*, I want to scream. But it won't matter. It's already out there. And judging by the look on Fal's face, she definitely heard it.

*Shit. This can't be good.*

On our way to the checkout, Fallon talks the whole time, and Echo nods at all the right places and says just enough to make her smile. I can tell she likes him. And Fallon St. James doesn't like anyone.

I hate that he's good at this. That he knows how to slip into people's lives so easily. And I really hate that even after knowing what he's capable of, I've gotten used to having him around.

By the time we're outside, the sun is lower, and the air is cooler. Echo carries our bags to my car, pops the trunk, and loads the groceries without asking. Fallon gives me a look when he finishes, wanting me to say something to him, but all I can do is shake my head. She has no idea how much danger we're in right now.

"Well, thanks for the help." Fallon says, offering Echo a smile before climbing into the passenger seat. "It was nice meeting you."

As soon as her door shuts, the energy between us shifts.

"I like her." He says, his voice low so that only I can hear it.

"I don't care." I whisper back.

"You should. It's important that your future husband and your best friend get along."

My jaw visibly drops.

"You're insane." I say, shaking my head. "And you need to stop."

"Stop what?"

"This." I hiss, flinging my hand between the two of us. "You. Us. We aren't a thing."

"We are. You just haven't accepted it yet."

"I'm serious, Echo."

"I am too." He pulls back just enough to look me in the eye. "Yesterday wasn't a mistake, Bambi. And you know it."

"It can't happen again."

"Why not?"

"Because you're—" I struggle to find words that don't sound completely insane. "Because this is wrong. All of it. You're stalking me. You assaulted Josh. You—"

"Saved you from a panic attack and removed a man who wouldn't respect your boundaries?" He asks, smoothly. "Yeah. Real terrible behavior on my part."

"That's not the point—"

"Then what is?" He cups my face, forcing me to meet his gaze. "Tell me, Bambi. What are you so afraid of?"

*You.* I want to say. *I'm afraid of you. But not in a way that makes sense. I'm afraid of how badly I still want you even when you've made it clear to me how dangerous you are.*

"I have to go." I say instead, pulling away from his touch. "Fallon's waiting."

He lets me move past him, but before I can open my door, he stops it with his hand. "When you think about me." He says, leaning in close so that his warm, minty breath fans across my ear. "Remember that I'm thinking about you, too. Constantly." His thumb strokes the side of my face. "And Bambi, just so you know, the next time I get you alone, I'm not leaving until you admit what this is."

Then he steps back and turns away.

I climb into the car on shaky legs and don't let myself look at him again as I put my keys in the ignition.

"So..." Fallon starts as soon as the car moves. "Bambi, huh?"

I roll my eyes. "It's just a dumb nickname he gave me. It doesn't mean anything."

"I hate to state the obvious, but he's hot."

I don't respond.

"Like, unfairly hot." She continues. "And clearly into you."

"Don't start."

"D, that man was eye-fucking you like crazy." She says, biting back a smile. "And you were totally eye-fucking him back."

"I was not." I say, even though I know that's a lie. "Besides, he's just a friend."

Fallon nods slowly, but I can tell she doesn't believe me. "Well, for what it's worth, I like him. And I never like any of the assholes you date."

*Only because she doesn't know him.*

Fallon keeps talking about him on the rest of the drive home, but I'm only half listening. All I can think about is the feel of his hand on my face. The sound of his voice in my ear. And the promise in his words.

*The next time I get you alone, I'm not leaving until you admit what this is.*

The thing is, I know exactly what this is, because it's all

we'll ever be. *Friends.* Anything more than that doesn't work for me.

He can have my body. He can have my attention. He can even have this twisted attraction to him I can't seem to shake. But I won't fall in love with him. *I can't.* So whatever this thing between us is, it ends before it becomes that. It has to.

# CHAPTER THIRTEEN

Dahlia

The cycling studio smells like rubber and serious regret, which is appropriate because I'm deeply questioning why I let Fallon talk me into this.

I push through the exit doors behind her on overcooked spaghetti legs, squinting against the afternoon sun. My hair is a disaster, sweat-soaked and pasted to my forehead, and my vagina feels like it's been kicked into oblivion. The only thing motivating me to move right now is the promise of a pedicure and the knowledge that I'll get sixty magical minutes with that mother-fucking massage chair.

Fallon is walking ahead of me, pulling her hair loose as she scrolls through her phone looking absolutely flawless and completely unbothered by the fact that we just spent forty-five minutes getting our asses handed to us by a woman named Lexi who has probably never experienced a negative emotion in her life.

I'm about to ask Fallon if she'll just leave me here and pull the car around for me when I spot a familiar face a few feet ahead of us.

Echo is sitting at a table just outside the entrance with two smoothies in front of him. He's dressed in all black, as always, with a fitted t-shirt, jeans, and a pair of boots.

It's annoying that he's even more pretty in the sunlight.

As soon as he spots us approaching, he stands up and holds a smoothie in my direction. "Mango Mayhem." He says. "With coconut cream."

I glare at him as I slowly reach for it.

"How did you—" I start, then think better of it and take a sip of the smoothie instead.

Asking him how he knew we'd be here is just begging for trouble. And who knows what the hell he'll say in front of Fallon. Echo has no problem dropping truth bombs around me, which would be kind of admirable if it weren't for the fact that his truth is absolutely psychotic.

He hands Fallon the other smoothie, and she eagerly plucks it from his hand and takes a long sip. "Ooh. And you got me a Strawberry Oasis?" She says, pointing at him. "You. I like."

Echo laughs, and the deep timbre of his voice reverberates through me, as if it's on a fucking mission to turn me on.

"You two hungry for real food?" He asks, looking between the two of us.

"Starving." Fallon says immediately.

"There's a great sushi place around the corner." He says, nodding towards it. "My treat."

Fallon takes another sip of her smoothie and gives Echo an emphatic nod.

*Shit.* This is bad. The last time I saw him, he told me the next time he got me alone he wasn't leaving until I admitted what this is. No way in hell am I going to agree to go anywhere with him, even if Fallon is there as the buffer.

"Fal," I say, grabbing her elbow and stopping her midstride.

"Hmm?" She hums, her lips still wrapped around her straw.

"Pedicures," I say, holding her gaze. "You promised, remember?"

Fallon scrunches up her nose and waves a hand at me. "Oh, we can do that after. Let's eat first—"

"Or… we can eat after." I insist, tightening my grip.

Fallon's eyes flick from my face to the hand on her elbow, and a slow knowing smile spreads across her face.

"Right." She says slowly, flashing him an apologetic smile. "Sorry, dude. We'll have to raincheck. Pedicures are calling our name."

I release her elbow and nod my head at Echo as I take another sip of my smoothie.

*Phew*. Crisis averted. No alone time, no uncomfortable conversations, no having to look him in the eye while my body remembers things my brain is actively trying to forget.

"Unless, of course," Fallon adds, flashing a smile at me, "you want to come with us?"

I suck in a breath and break into a fit of coughing as I nearly choke on a chunk of mango.

*Fucking Fallon.*

I glare at her and I swear to God, I've never wanted to strangle my best friend more.

"Sure," Echo says, fighting a smile. "Why not?"

"You can't—" I sputter, looking between Fallon and Echo, who both seem to be enjoying this way too fucking much. "We were supposed to—" I say, shaking my head. "Fine. That's fine."

THE NAIL SALON IS THREE BLOCKS DOWN FROM OUR CYCLING class and small enough that the three of us take up most of the pedicure chairs along the back wall. Fallon picks the seat to my left and immediately dives into conversation with her technician about a show they've both been watching.

Echo sits to my right and looks around the salon with the same sharp, assessing attention he gives every room he enters. Which is kind of funny, considering the shop is drenched in pastel pink and is probably the least dangerous place he's ever stepped foot in.

The technician helping him pulls out the color samples and hands them to him. He looks at them for a second, then turns to me.

"What's your favorite color, Bambi?"

I furrow my brow. "Why does that matter?"

"Because I need to pick one." He says, his gaze dragging over my face. "And I don't make decisions without factoring you in."

I roll my eyes and try to ignore the way his words make my stomach flutter.

"You can just get clear."

He tilts his head. "Is clear your favorite color?"

"Of course not."

"Then that would be pointless."

I audibly sigh and point to the pastel yellow color that's been my favorite color ever since I was little. "That one."

"Buttercream." He says softly, staring at it like he's committing it to memory. "Buttercream is it."

I glare at him. "You're really going to put that on your toes?"

He smirks. "Of course."

"Why?"

His eyes lock on mine, and my stomach does that stupid

little flutter thing that I hate. "Because I want you, Bambi." He pauses, licking his lips. "On me. All the time."

I swallow hard. "That's not intense at all."

Echo smiles. "Intense would be carving your name into my fucking chest. This is me showing restraint."

On my left, Fallon chokes on her smoothie, then tries and fails to disguise it as a cough.

I don't look at her. I already know what her face is doing, and that so will not help the situation right now. I open my mouth, then immediately slam it shut.

*How do I even respond to that?*

<hr>

AN HOUR LATER, THE THREE OF US ARE WALKING DOWN THE street with our toes freshly polished, and Fallon is checking her phone with that focused frown she gets when something is going on at work.

"Everything okay?" I ask.

"Yeah, it's just—" She looks up. "I'm on call today and it looks like they need me there ASAP."

Fallon is pretty chill about most things, but when it comes to her work as an ER nurse, she takes what she does very seriously. After watching her work her ass off for the last four years, I don't think it's just a job for her anymore. It's a calling.

"I totally get it," I say, nodding my head. "Do you have time to drop me off first?"

Fallon winces. "Shit, I forgot we rode together." She says, running a hand through her long blonde hair. "The hospital's the opposite way, so it'll add like an hour to my drive. Do you mind hanging out in the waiting room for a bit?"

"How long is a bit?"

"I don't know, an hour. Maybe two?"

"I can take her." Echo offers.

Both of our heads swivel in his direction. I got so wrapped up in the conversation with Fallon that I completely forgot he was still standing there with us. I turn back towards Fallon and wave a hand. "Fal, you go ahead. I'll just grab an Uber or something."

Echo crosses his muscular arms across his chest, and I try not to notice how biteable his shoulders look in that slutty ass t-shirt he's wearing. "I said I'll take you home, Bambi."

"I'm okay." I say automatically, flashing him a tight smile. "Really, Uber is fine."

Echo smirks. "You'd rather pay a stranger than take a free ride from me?"

"Yup." I retort, emphasizing the 'p' with a pop.

"That makes no sense."

"It doesn't need to."

Fallon's eyes light up as they ping-pong between me and Echo, like she's watching the most enthralling tennis match she's ever seen. "You know," she says, pursing her lips. "I'm not one to blindly agree with a man, but he has a point, D."

I cut my eyes at the traitor who was formerly known as my best friend. "Don't you have somewhere to be?"

Fallon laughs. "I do." She says, pulling me in for a quick hug. "Love you. Text me when you get home."

And with that, Fallon trots off, leaving me alone with the one person in the world I shouldn't be alone with.

"Come on." Echo says, nodding his head in the direction of his car.

"I told you, I'm Ubering."

"Bambi." He says, his voice taking on that faintly amused tone it always does when he thinks I'm being unreasonable.

"Echo." I reply, mocking him right back.

He stares at me. I stare back. A woman pushing a stroller squeezes past us on the sidewalk, and we both instinctively step aside, then go right back to staring at each other.

"I'm not going to do anything." He says.

"I didn't say you were."

"Then what's the problem?"

The problem is that the last time I saw you, you pressed your mouth to my ear and told me you weren't leaving until I admitted what this is. The problem is that I've been thinking about that every single day since, and I still don't have an answer, not one I can accept, anyway. The problem is that you might not plan on doing anything, but I might, and I can't seem to control myself around you.

"There is no problem." I reply cooly. "I just prefer Uber."

"You prefer Uber," he repeats.

"Yes."

"To a free ride in a nicer car."

"Yes."

"From someone you know."

"That's a bit of a stretch, isn't it?"

His mouth does that thing where it almost becomes a smile but doesn't quite get there, then he reaches into his pocket and pulls out his keys.

"Open the app." He says, nodding at my phone. "Let's check the wait time. If it's over five minutes, you're coming with me."

"Why five minutes?"

"Because I think you can keep yourself alive for five minutes, but any longer is asking for trouble."

I glare at him.

"Five minutes, Bambi. Check."

I look down at my phone and pull up the app.

Eleven minutes.

*Fuck.*

"Well?" He asks.

I roll my eyes and slip the phone back into my pocket.

"Fine," I sigh, "but I'm not making conversation with you."

The corner of his mouth ticks up. "Okay."

"And you're taking me straight home."

"Of course."

"And—"

"Bambi." He says, cutting me off gently. "It's just a ride."

I look at him for one more second, searching for the angle and not finding one.

"Fine." I mutter, falling into step beside him. "But if we get into an accident and you fucking kill me, I'm coming back to haunt your ass."

# CHAPTER FOURTEEN

Dahlia

The city moves past us in a blur of autumn foliage and colorful storefronts. And even though it's the first time we've been alone together since the grocery store incident two weeks ago, I'm doing totally fine.

I'm not thinking about how good he smells, or how hot he looks driving this ridiculously sexy car, and I'm definitely not thinking about what happened the last time the two of us were alone together.

*Nope.* Not thinking about that at all. *Did I mention I'm a goddamn liar?*

I shift in my seat, and as my eyes look at everything but him, they catch on a book sitting in the center console. It's flipped over, but recognition clicks immediately.

It's Darkfever. The book Echo bought from me the first time he came to the store. The spine is creased, the pages are frayed, and there's a receipt being used as a bookmark somewhere around the three quarter mark.

I stare at it for a second, then flick my eyes towards Echo and lean forward to turn the volume down.

"You're actually reading it." I say, sneaking a peek at his side profile.

Echo takes his eyes off the road for a split second to glance at the console and nods.

"Why?" I ask, a little more bluntly than I mean to.

"You said it was one of your favorites." He shrugs. "I wanted to know why."

"Did you figure it out?"

"I think so."

I wait a few seconds for him to elaborate, and when I realize he isn't going to, I roll my eyes and pivot in my seat to face him. "So are you going to tell me... or?"

"You like Mac because you're just as reckless and stubborn as she is."

I open my mouth, ready to refute his ridiculous claim, but when I stop to think about it, the words die on my tongue.

*Okay, he isn't totally off base there.*

"And," he adds, pausing as a smug smirk spreads across his unfairly pretty face. "You have a danger kink so you definitely want to fuck a Barrons."

My mouth falls open and heat spreads up my neck.

"I'm sorry, what?"

Echo's eyes never leave the road. "You heard me."

"I—" I pause, scrambling for a good rebuttal. "I do not have a danger kink, and Barrons is the male lead. He's literally designed to be attractive to the reader."

Echo nods his head like I'm a child he's trying to humor. "Whatever you say, Bambi."

"Not to mention, it's perfectly normal to find a dangerous fictional character attractive." I retort, crossing my arms across my chest. "It's not like I'd find that hot in real life."

Echo glances at me. "You don't?"

"No."

He cocks a brow. "Not even a little?"

"No," I say firmly.

His gaze slides back to the road, but the corner of his mouth lifts. "Interesting."

"Not really," I scoff, turning to look out the window again. "It's common sense."

"Explain something to me, then." He says, pulling the car to a stop at a red light.

I turn to face him. "What."

He taps the steering wheel with his thumbs and looks up thoughtfully, as if he's trying to form the right words.

My eyes skim over the planes of his face and linger on the muscles working in his throat.

*Ugh. Even his neck is hot.*

"If danger isn't sexy to you," he says slowly, locking his eyes on mine, "then why do you think about me when you touch yourself?"

All the moisture on my tongue dissipates as my brain fires jumbled thoughts off in rapid succession.

*How does he...*

*Why does he...*

*What kind of fucking question is that?*

*The kind I won't be answering truthfully.*

"I don't." I reply flatly, doing my best to keep the emotion out of my voice. "So don't flatter yourself."

"Now's not the time to start lying to each other, Bambi." He says, keeping his eyes on me. "Answer the question honestly this time."

The light turns green, but Echo makes no move to start driving again. He just keeps his eyes firmly locked on mine, even as the cars behind us start honking their horns.

"Echo, it's green." I say, glancing at the road. "Drive."

"As you wish."

Echo takes his foot off the brake and presses the accelerator, but his gaze still hasn't moved from me.

"What are you doing?" I say, flicking my eyes between him and the road in front of us. "Stop looking at me and put your eyes on the road."

"No."

"What do you mean, no?"

"I'm not looking away until you give me an honest answer."

"I am being honest."

"You're not, and you know exactly how I know that."

It dawns on me then. Echo watches me. He has been since we met, and he's never once tried to hide it.

*Motherfucker.*

That night. That night I stupidly dry-humped him and felt so incredibly wound up after he left that I had no choice but to finish myself. *Fuck.* Did I moan his name? Yeah, I'm pretty sure I did.

I stare at Echo, and I hate that the smug smile on his face makes him look both punchable and fuckable.

*No way.*

No way am I going to admit that I did that. Even if he did watch me do it, acknowledging it out loud would be catastrophic for my pride, or at least, the little of it I have left when it comes to him.

A horn blares, and a silver sedan screeches to a halt on our right as Echo runs a red light and zooms past it.

"Jesus Christ, you're going to get us killed."

"I won't," he says, flashing a smile at me, "but you might, if you don't answer me honestly."

"Echo, this isn't funny."

"All the more reason to tell the truth."

"Fine." I snap, white-knuckling the overhead handle as

he blows through another red light. "I have thought about you. You're attractive, okay? Is that what you wanted to hear?"

"Yes." He says easily, his eyes finally returning to the road. "That's exactly what I wanted to hear."

I release a breath and sink back into my seat, as relieved as I am mortified.

The rest of the drive passes in silence, but oddly enough, it isn't uncomfortable, which might be the most annoying thing about Echo. He has this infuriating ability to make me comfortable in his presence, even when he's the last person in the world I should feel comfortable with.

We pull onto my street, and I'm already rehearsing my exit in my head. If I can just keep it short, civil, and clean, I might be able to get out of this car with at least a little of my dignity intact.

Echo parks in front of my building, cuts the engine, and gets out of the car.

I reach for the door handle to follow him, but before I can, the automatic lock shifts into place.

Narrowing my eyes, I watch Echo through the windshield as he rounds the front of the car and stops on my side to pull the door open.

I stare up at him. "I'm capable of opening my own door."

"I know." He replies, giving me his hand. "Humor me, Bambi."

I hold his gaze for a second, then reluctantly reach for his hand. His touch is strong and so much warmer than I expected.

"There you go," he says, helping me out of the car, "was that so bad?"

*It wasn't.* At all. And that's part of the problem.

Standing to my full height, I toss my hair back, and I

make it approximately one step before Echo's arm shoots out to cage me against the car and the open passenger door.

"What are you doing?" I ask, mildly impressed with how steady my voice sounds.

"Gloating."

I jerk my head back. "About what?"

"I told you the next time I got you alone I'd get you to admit what this was."

I furrow my brow. "I didn't admit anything."

"You admitted you're attracted to me."

"So." I shake my head. "Half of the world's population is probably attracted to you. That doesn't mean anything."

"It means something to me."

"Well, it shouldn't," I say flatly. "It's not like I have feelings for you."

He tilts his head, studying me, and he doesn't even look slightly discouraged.

"You don't have feelings for me *yet*." He says, emphasizing his last word. "But you will."

"So you can predict the future now?"

"It's not a prediction. It's an inevitability. The first hurdle is already out of the way and now you've gone and exposed your weakness."

"What weakness?"

Echo leans in and his lips brush against the sensitive shell of my ear. His minty breath cascades down my neck, and I'm trying and failing to slow my breathing.

"Me." He whispers. "And my cock that you can't stop thinking about."

The heat that flows through me is immediate and involuntary and absolutely mortifying.

I swallow hard as his mouth gently curves against my skin. He pulls back to look at me, and his eyes are dark and entirely too amused. I'm completely out of sorts, and he seems to be enjoying every second of this.

"Off you go, Bambi." He says, dropping his arm and finally letting me free.

I push off the car door and walk towards my building on shaky legs. Every single part of me wants to look back at him. Wants to see if he's just as affected as I am from that little interaction. But I'm sure he's watching, and if we make eye contact again, there's a good chance I'll end up doing something I'll regret.

I make it into the lobby, up the elevator, and all the way to my apartment before I let out a long, shaking breath and press my forehead against the door.

He barely touched me. Just lightly grazed my skin with his lips, and somehow it was the hottest thing I've ever experienced in my life.

The heat that pooled between my legs hasn't faded and my heart is still rioting wildly in my chest. I run my fingers over the place he touched me and squeeze my eyes shut.

*Maybe he's right.*

*Maybe I do have a danger kink.*

# CHAPTER FIFTEEN

*Echo*

BAMBI WANTS ME.

She didn't admit it freely, and she tried to minimize the words as soon as they left her mouth. But she said it, and more importantly, she knows I heard it.

Since we met, Bambi's body has been telling me everything her mouth refuses to, and her confession today finally confirmed what I already knew.

She wants *me*.

Now the only question is, what do I plan on doing with that information?

---

IT'S JUST PAST 2AM WHEN I ENTER THE UNDERGROUND garage and as expected, mine is the only car circling the lot. I pull into a spot on the lower level and kill the engine before reaching across to the passenger seat to grab the bouquet I had customized just for her.

It's a dense arrangement of flowers and greenery filled

with roses, tulips, and dahlias in varying shades of her favorite color: buttercream yellow.

She gave me an inch today. I intend to take so much more. So the least I can do is soften the blow with something that'll make her smile.

I ride the elevator up to the fourth floor and step out into the quiet hallway with the bouquet at my side.

My pace slows as I approach Bambi's door, and for a moment, I stand there, letting my loafers sink into her plush doormat.

My fingers graze against the surface of the door, and I can almost feel her pull through the inches of plywood. She's in there, probably fast asleep, and deeply unaware of how close I am to her. So vulnerable. So unassuming. So fucking *mine*.

Before I get too ahead of myself, I step away from her door and force myself to keep walking down the hall. I come to a stop in front of the apartment next to hers, and after making sure the hallway is still empty, I reach into my pocket, grab my key, and carefully unlock the door.

Bambi doesn't know I've owned this unit for over three weeks now. I thought she might've caught on when showed up on her 4th floor balcony, but she never even questioned it. It was a bit of an impulse purchase, but I needed the privacy, and keeping an eye on her from a distance just wasn't enough anymore. Fortunately, the unit was already vacant, which made things considerably cleaner.

As soon as I'm inside, I kick off my shoes and shrug off my jacket before hanging it on the coat rack. The apartment is quiet tonight, and the only source of light is the city's glow bleeding in through the patio door. Stepping deeper into the living room, I set the bouquet down on the coffee table and loosen my tie as I sink into the leather sectional.

Grabbing the remote, I turn on the big screen and the live feed of Bambi's bedroom comes into focus.

She's on her side, facing the back patio, with her arm folded under her and a frown marring her otherwise smooth face. The light filtering through her curtains catches the line of her jaw, and the slow rise and fall of her shoulder beneath the duvet.

She's out cold.

I stand up, grab the bouquet off the coffee table, and head for my patio door.

***

HER SLIDING GLASS DOOR IS OPEN WHEN I ARRIVE, LEAVING the flimsy screen door as the only barrier between her and the outside world.

She does this every night. Leaves it open like fresh air is worth the risk, like nothing bad could ever find its way through her fourth-floor patio door. It used to frustrate me, and in some ways, it still does. But now that I have a place of my own that keeps me within steps of her, I can rest a little easier knowing I'm right there if she ever needs me.

I slide the door open and step inside.

The room smells faintly of that peach sugar lotion she always applies after her shower. It wraps around me the second I cross the threshold, and my eyes find the bottle on her nightstand immediately. I cross the room before I make the conscious decision to, and pocket it.

She'll eventually notice it's gone. She'll reach for it the way she always does, come up empty, and know exactly who took it.

*Good.* She should think about me. I think about her constantly.

I glance at her bed and, as usual, Bambi is sleeping on her stomach with one leg kicked out from underneath the covers and both of her arms folded beneath her head. She's dreaming. The moonlight spilling in highlights the way her lashes flutter against her cheeks as her face twitches.

Even if she weren't deeply under, I wouldn't be worried. There's no version of this situation where I get caught, and even if there were, I'm not sure it would change anything. Bambi knows exactly what I am, and she's attracted to me in spite of it, or more likely, because of it.

I take my time as I move through her room. I've seen it plenty of times through the camera lens, but being in here, experiencing it firsthand, feels different. More intimate. Still, I move through it the same way I move through everything that belongs to me, unbothered and without apology.

I round the foot of the bed and set the bouquet on her nightstand. Then I step back and look at it.

The flowers are almost luminous in the dark. I had the florist spend the better part of an hour getting the arrangement right because I needed it to say something specific.

*I know you.* Not the version you perform for everyone else. The real one. The one you think no one else can see. I see you, Bambi. I always do.

My eyes move from the bouquet back to her, and I can't help but stare. Her hair fans across her pillow, and her lips are slightly parted. She looks soft like this, unguarded in a way she never is with me. She gives me her anger, her frustration, and even her lust, but the softness she reserves for herself.

*Not for long, though.*

I reach out and let my fingers hover just above her cheek. A breath away. Close enough to feel the warmth rising off her skin. Close enough that if she stirred, if she turned even slightly in her sleep, my skin would be on hers.

She's so deeply asleep that I probably could touch her right now and she wouldn't even feel it. I could taste and explore every inch of that beautiful fucking body of hers, and she'd wake up in the morning none-the-wiser.

But the thing is, when I touch Bambi, I *want* her to feel it. And taking from her won't feel nearly as good as when she looks me in the eye and gives it to me of her own volition. I want her, yes. But I want her to want me even more, and I won't settle for anything less.

I drop my hand and take one last look at the flowers on her nightstand, the buttercream arrangement she'll see as soon as she opens her eyes. Then, I turn around and leave her room the same way I came. Silently, smoothly, and without a single ounce of remorse.

# CHAPTER SIXTEEN

DAHLIA

I WAKE UP BURNING. MY LEGS ARE TANGLED IN AN INTRICATE web of sheets that are way too fucking hot, and my whole body is slick with a thin layer of sweat. I take a breath, and the air I pull in feels sticky and humid, so reminiscent of the hot summer nights I grew up with in the south, that for a split second, I think I might be dreaming. But when I flick my eyes open and find my dark bedroom staring back at me, I know I'm awake.

I flop over and glance at the clock on the wall. 4:30am. It should still be cool out, so why the fuck is it so hot in here? I glance at my patio door and find it completely shut.

*What the hell?*

I always sleep with it open. Fallon runs cold, so she blasts the heat at night, and the only thing that stops me from roasting in my sleep is that door that should be fucking open.

I frown at it for a second, then grumble and haul myself out of bed. I must've forgotten to do it. It's a stupid mistake, but it honestly tracks because I've been making stupid moves all day. Hitching a ride home with my stalker, being one of them.

Still half-asleep, I pad across the room, grab the handle, and jerk it open. Cool air rushes in immediately, and I sigh with relief as it blows across my overheated skin.

I spin back around and trudge forward, as relieved as I am annoyed that my sleep was interrupted.

I'm about to flop back into bed when my eyes catch on something sitting on my nightstand. Flowers. A shit ton of them. Wrapped in a silk ribbon and all in varying shades of soft yellow. My favorite color. My stomach drops through the floor.

*What the actual fuck?*

I glare at the flowers, completely baffled. They have to be a figment of my imagination. Some hallucination my par-cooked brain thought up and planted there just to punish me for failing to protect it from Fallon's nightly broiling session.

*Yeah,* I think to myself, *it's the middle of the night and I'm tired as hell. I must be imagining it.*

I let my brain latch onto that thought as I close my eyes and crawl right back into bed.

I'm not a complete idiot. I know exactly what I'm avoiding, but right now I'm tired, and I can stomach the thought of me having delusions and still fall asleep. What I can't sleep through is the alternative, because it's scarier in a very different way.

THREE HOURS LATER MY ALARM GOES OFF AND I WAKE UP TO the bouquet exactly where it was before, looking even more out of place in the daylight.

*Fuck.* Definitely real. And definitely from Echo.

I glare at the obnoxiously pretty flowers and clench my jaw. Of course they're perfect. Of course, they're anything but generic and are exactly the kind of flowers I'd want. And of course they came from one man I should be staying away from.

I reach for my phone and debate on calling Echo to tell him exactly where he can shove the stems he left for me, but then I think about what my stupid heart will do the minute I hear his voice, and I change my mind, deciding to text him instead.

> You were in my room last night.

His three dots appear almost immediately.

Good morning to you too, Bambi.

> Echo...

Yes?

> You broke into my apartment.

You left the door open for me.

I stare at the screen and my eye twitches. So I did open it last night after all.

> No, I didn't.

Did you find them?

I look up at the bouquet, then back at my phone.

> Obviously.

And?

I press my lips together and glare at the flowers again, searching for an answer hidden somewhere in their petals.

I should just throw them away. Knowing him, he probably laced the ribbon with some kind of neurotoxin. Either that, or he purposely left the thorns on it to force me to take part in some twisted blood bond with him.

I didn't want these.

I *don't* want these.

Don't do that again.

His reply is instant.

Lock your door, and I won't be able to.

I exit our text thread and toss my phone onto the mattress.

Then I get up, walk to the kitchen, and spend a genuinely embarrassing amount of time looking for the right vase. I fill it with water, carry it back to my room, and put the flowers in it.

They really are the most beautiful flowers I've ever seen.

# CHAPTER SEVENTEEN

DAHLIA

ECHO HAS VISITED ME EVERY NIGHT THIS WEEK.

I wish I could say I'm outraged by this. Hell, I wish I could even say I'm surprised. But I'm the one who keeps leaving the door unlocked for him, like some kind of fucked-up invitation I can't stop extending.

Every morning I wake up to evidence that he was in my private space. A missing hair tie. The book on my nightstand shifted into a different position. A replacement bouquet so that the flowers he gave me never wilt, which would be a ridiculously romantic gesture, if I weren't sure he's only doing it to fuck with me.

He always does little things that make me question my sanity. Like he's trying to see how long it'll take for me to lose my mind completely. Turns out it's six days.

Six days of him watching me while I sleep and not doing a single thing about it. I don't know what I expected. No, that's a lie. I know exactly what I expected, even if I'm not ready to admit it to him.

After six nights of waking up with proof that my stalker

was close enough to touch me and still chose not to, I'm done waiting.

Tonight, Echo will give me exactly what I want, and I won't have to say a single word.

Since Echo started watching me, I've made it a habit to get dressed in the bathroom, purely for my own sanity. Tonight, though, I slipped back into my room, freshly show-ered with nothing but a towel on.

Now I'm standing by my bed, preparing myself to let the fabric fall to the floor. As soon as I let go, the cool air hits me and goosebumps spread across my skin. Echo's probably already watching, but I don't let myself focus on that. Denial isn't healthy, but neither is trying to bait your stalker into fucking you while you sleep.

I pull back the covers and slip into bed, surprised by how good the buttery silk sheets feel against my skin. I've never slept naked before. It always felt like a risk that wasn't worth taking. I mean, what if an emergency happened in the middle of the night, or God forbid someone broke in? Would I really want a stranger to stumble in on me, butt-ass-naked? Hell no. But apparently I'm cool with a man that I know is a killer doing just that.

I'm not sure how much time passes while I lie there, barely covered by a corner of the sheet pretending to sleep, but it's long enough that I start to wonder if maybe he won't show up tonight. Which would be both a relief and absolutely infuriating.

Then the breeze from outside lulls and I know he's here.

I keep my breathing slow and even as let my body go limp. In. out. In. out. And envision myself as someone who's deeply asleep and definitely not vibrating with anticipation.

Echo's footsteps are so quiet that I'd miss them if I wasn't listening this hard. But I catch them, soft and slow, moving through the dark as if he's memorized every inch of my room.

Then he stops and everything goes quiet.

He's looking at me. I can feel it. And based on the fact that he hasn't moved an inch, he's either stunned into a stupor or admiring the view.

A few minutes pass, and I'm starting to think he might just stand there staring at me all night, which was so not the point of this.

So I decide to push him.

I shift my body slightly, pretending to be in the throes of deep sleep, and I hear him suck in a breath as my exposed breasts jiggle.

The sound reverberates straight to my pussy and within seconds I'm wet.

His hand reaches out and settles over my breast so carefully that for a moment I think I'm imagining it. His touch is so light, so barely there, that it's borderline maddening. I want him to touch me harder, but I can feel the hesitation seeping through his skin.

I let out a slow, sleepy sound and lean into his touch slightly, letting his hand palm my breast even more.

His hand responds immediately, squeezing it tighter as his thumb slides out to graze my nipple.

My breath hitches at the contact, and I inwardly wince.

*Shit.*

That wasn't even close to the sound a sleeping person would make, and we both know it.

Echo's hand stills, and I pretend to groan in my sleep, hoping it'll convince him to keep going.

*I don't want him to stop.*

*I never want him to stop.*

His thumb grazes my nipple again, slower this time, and

the breath that leaves me this time is more convincing. I melt into his touch and feel the weight of his body settle next to me on my bed.

He pulls the sheets off me, and I fight the urge to shiver as his hand leaves my breast and begins a slow, agonizing trail down. Over my ribs, past the curve of my waist, and down my hips.

My thighs are already pressed together when his hand finds them. And when he slips his hand between them, my legs go pliant in a way that I'm sure no sleeping person's ever has. He parts them painfully slowly, and exposes my slick center to the cool air.

"Look at you." He whispers, running his finger gently over the seam of my cunt. "Even in sleep, you're soaked for me."

My lips twitch.

*It's working.*

*It's actually working.*

The mattress shifts as he stands, and I track his movement through the dark behind my closed eyelids, straining to figure out what he's doing. Then I hear his belt unbuckle, followed by the unmistakable sound of a zipper sliding.

*Oh my god.*

*Oh my god, it actually worked.*

Every muscle in my body is screaming at me to open my eyes, to watch him strip, and to stop pretending so I can fully experience the moment I've been waiting for. But I can't. Not without revealing how badly I want this. So I keep my face slack and try my best to keep my breathing slow, even as my heart hammers in my chest.

The mattress dips on either side of me, and I can sense him standing over me. He's so close that I can feel the heat radiating off his body and can smell that familiar warm, woody scent that I've stopped pretending I don't love.

His minty breath fans across my face, and my mouth literally salivates with anticipation.

*He's so close.*

*So fucking close.*

Every nerve ending in my body is on fire, and it takes every ounce of self-control I have not to reach out and pull him on top of me.

He inches closer, and when he finally speaks again, his lips brush against my ear and send a shiver down my spine.

"If you want my cock, you're going to have to open your eyes and beg for it."

# CHAPTER EIGHTEEN

*Echo*

"If you want my cock, you're going to have to open your eyes and beg for it."

The second my words land, a deep blush spreads across Bambi's cheeks and her breathing picks up dramatically.

She was never asleep. I've known that from the moment I walked in and saw her lying there. Bambi snores when she sleeps. It's a small, soft sound. One that I've memorized after weeks of watching her. But tonight, I walked in and her room was completely silent.

That was new.

So was the fact that she was sleeping naked.

From that point on, I knew exactly what she wanted, and I was willing to play along with her little charade to a certain extent. But I won't be taking her like this.

When Bambi and I fuck, I want her full buy-in. No plausible deniability and no pretending she's just a victim of my deviant obsession. She knows exactly what she's doing, and if she wants this to go any further, she needs to admit it.

Even if it's fucking killing me not to keep going.

I let out a deep groan as I stroke my hard cock and take in every naked inch of her body.

The blush on her cheeks deepens, and she slacks her body even more. I'm sure she thinks if she commits to the bit hard enough, I'll let her get away with it and keep going. I won't.

"Bammbiiii."

No response.

"Hm. Guess you don't want my cock inside of you after all."

I back away from her, even though it physically pains me to do it, and I start pulling my clothes back on. I meant what I said. I'm not going any further until she admits she wants this. So if it ends here, then it ends here.

"Don't you fucking touch that zipper."

My head snaps up, and I find Bambi glaring at me, looking equal parts furious, mortified, and turned on, which, I must admit, is one of my favorite combinations on her.

"So you are awake?"

She rolls her eyes at me as she sits up, and the horny bastard in me can't help but stare at her bouncing tits.

"I'll admit that I want this," she says, "if you agree it doesn't mean anything. We're just two friends getting this out of our system, and after tonight, things go back to normal."

She says it so confidently that for a second, even I almost believe her. But Bambi knows we've never been "just friends", so the fact that she's trying to cling onto that label, even now, almost makes me laugh. Denial keeps her comfortable, so I'll let her have this. At least for now.

"Whatever you say, Bambi."

She opens her mouth, ready to argue her point, but when my words click, the fight leaves her eyes almost immediately.

Her brow furrows, and I can tell she's already starting to overthink this. Probably questioning why I gave in so easily and wondering if there's some kind of loophole I found to get out of her little terms and conditions.

There isn't. This woman could take everything she wanted from me, and I'd probably thank her for the privilege. I'm that fucking gone for her.

"So…" I drawl, tilting my head at her.

She looks up at me, and I'm suddenly painfully aware of how naked she is. "So what?"

"I agreed to your terms, now it's time to agree to mine."

"I did agree."

"Not fully."

Realization dawns on her, and she levels me with a look of outrage. I stand firm on what I said and stare right back at her. After a little silent standoff, she lets out an exaggerated sigh and finally moves to speak. "Echo, will you-"

"Ah. Ah. Ah." I tsk. "I want it done properly. On your knees, Bambi."

Her lips flatten into a thin line, and she cuts her eyes at me as she reluctantly slips out of bed.

"You're an asshole."

"That I am," I say smoothly. "Now get on your knees and beg for this cock."

She takes her sweet time lowering herself to knees, and by the time she's knelt down in front of me, her expression has gone from very annoyed to downright sinful.

She inches closer to me, and when the aroma of her peach-scented skin hits me, it takes all the strength I have not to grab her by the hair and show her exactly what the fuck she does to me.

She looks up at me with those fuck-me almond-shaped eyes I dream about, and slowly licks her lips.

"Echo." She says, sliding my pants and my boxer briefs down my thighs. "Will you please give me some cock?"

Her eyes shift from my face to my dick, and the hunger I see in them is enough to drive me crazy.

"You can have whatever the fuck you want, beautiful."

She smiles up at me as she takes my thick cock in her hand and leans forward to slowly slide her tongue from the base all the way up to the tip.

I hiss through my teeth at the sensation, and my hand finds her hair instinctively. She wraps her lips around my cock, swirling her tongue, and I swear to god, for a second, my vision completely blacks out.

*She's so fucking good at this.*

Bambi takes her time exploring my cock. Licking and nibbling and sucking and stroking. All the while, watching my every reaction.

She's studying me the same way I've been studying her since the night we met, and *Jesus Christ*, she might be even better at it.

"Bambi." I groan, her name coming out way more strangled than I intended.

She hums against my cock and looks up at me, wild amusement shining in her eyes as she keeps sucking.

*Goddamn, she knows exactly what she's doing.*

I tighten my grip on her hair and pull her back before this ends earlier than either of us want it to.

She releases my cock with a pop and looks up at me, lips swollen, eyes dark. She almost made me come in under two minutes, and the smile she flashes me tells me she's fucking proud of herself for it. I decide, right then and there, that I'm going to spend the rest of the night making her deeply regret that smile.

"Get on the fucking bed, Bambi. Now."

For once, she doesn't argue. She just gets to her feet, scurries over to the bed, and lies down on her back.

After slipping on a condom, I round the bed and drop down beside her.

"Come here." I say, reaching for her hand. "I want that beautiful cunt on my face."

She pulls her hand away and stares at me. "Absolutely not."

"Absolutely yes."

"Echo—"

"Bambi."

"I've never—" She gestures vaguely between her pussy and my face, which is really fucking adorable. "I don't know what I'm doing. I could hurt you."

I stare at her.

"I'm serious," she says, scowling at me. "What if I suffocate you?"

"Bambi, if I get the privilege of being suffocated by that beautiful cunt of yours, I promise you, I would be dying a very happy man. Now get the fuck over here."

She moves slowly, crawling over me and tracking my face like she's waiting for me to change my mind or give her a reason to change hers. She hovers just above me, her thighs bracketing my head, and I can feel the hesitation rolling off her in waves.

"Sit down, Bambi." I bite out, gripping her by her hips.

She lowers herself way too fucking slowly, and when I pull her the rest of the way down and flick my tongue against her clit, her whole body jolts.

Her hands fly to the headboard and she grips it tight, knuckles going white as I dig my fingers into her hips, and grind her sweet cunt against my face.

As I lap at her pussy, I feel her hesitation melt away. Her hips start moving on their own, and she moans unabashedly every time my tongue flicks her clit with just the right amount of pressure.

Her orgasm builds fast, and when she shatters on my tongue and curses my fucking name, pride roars in my chest.

*That's right, Bambi.*

*Tell everyone whose face you're riding.*

Her body goes slack above me, and I give her about two seconds to breathe before I sit up and lay her out onto her back.

I crawl over her, and as I nestle my cock between her trembling thighs, she looks up at me and swallows hard.

"Jesus Christ," she breathes, feeling the tip of my cock nudge against her entrance. "Did it—did it get even bigger?"

I look down at her and smirk, knowing it definitely fucking did.

"Jesus or not. The only man's name I want on your lips is mine."

I push inside her, and her eyes slam shut as her body adjusts to the size of me.

"Eyes on me, Bambi." I murmur, taking hold of her chin and tilting her face towards me.

Her eyes flutter open, and when they lock on mine, she sinks her teeth into her lower lip.

"Good fucking girl." I croon, slipping my thumb into her mouth as I slide into her again. "I want you to see exactly whose cock you're coming on."

Bambi holds my gaze as I pick up my pace, pushing into her deeper, faster, and harder. Her eyes roll in the back of her head a few times, but she never shuts them again.

We hold each other's gaze even when it gets hard to. Even when her breath turns to gasps and tears fill her pretty brown eyes. Even when her moans turn into screams and her nails claw against the old scars on my back. Even when my control finally snaps and I slam into her pussy so hard, we both come, cursing each other's names.

I stay there for a second, breathing hard, hovering over her as the last of my orgasm tears through me. Her body is still trembling beneath me, her breaths coming in thin, uneven pulls, and when I lift my head and look at her, she still doesn't look away.

So I keep looking at her. At her flushed skin. Her swollen mouth. At the tears still clinging to her lashes, and the softness in her glossy eyes.

Even like this, wrecked, breathless, and thoroughly fucked, she's still the most beautiful woman I've ever seen.

"You should probably go." She whispers, swallowing as her eyes shift to the patio door. "It's late and I've got work in the morning."

"Yeah." I nod, furrowing my brow. "Right."

I back off of her, and as soon as I'm out of bed, she pulls the sheet up over herself.

I find my clothes in the dark and get dressed slowly, listening for any sign that she's changed her mind. By the time I tug my shirt on, she's already turned away from me.

"Goodnight, Bambi." I say, hesitating near the door.

"Night." She says softly, not even bothering to look back.

I step out of her room and gently slide the door closed behind.

A few minutes ago, she let me bury myself inside of her, and we watched each other come. Now she won't even turn to look at me.

I've felt like an object my whole life. A weapon. A solution. A tool. Something to reach for when there's a problem, then set back down when the problem's gone. I know that feeling. I expect that feeling. I just never expected to feel it from her.

# CHAPTER NINETEEN

THE SECOND THE PATIO DOOR CLOSES, THE ROOM GOES painfully still, and the air feels colder than it did a minute ago. For a moment, I just lay there staring at the wall, listening to the sound of my own breathing.

*What the hell was that?*

Not the sex. I went into tonight knowing exactly what I wanted, and Echo more than delivered on my expectations.

I'm talking about that moment afterward.

The one where he stared into my eyes while he was still deep inside of me. The one where he didn't say anything, but the soft, almost reverent look on his face said everything. He was looking at me like this meant more to him than just sex. And for a second, it started to feel like more than sex for me, too. Then I panicked.

Was it a dick move to kick him out seconds after he came inside of me? Absolutely. But I didn't want either of us lying there in the dark, saying something stupid and turning one reckless decision into a much bigger mistake.

I sit up and drag both hands through my hair.

*I don't know what the hell is going on with me.*

I've done this before. Not with Echo, obviously, but the concept of hooking up with someone isn't new to me. I know how to keep sex simple. I've kept it simple with men who said all the right things and looked great on paper. Men who were charming as hell, and who were significantly less dangerous than he is. Keeping feelings out of it has never been an issue for me.

*So why is my stomach twisting itself into knots right now?*

I fall back against the pillow and stare up at the ceiling. Maybe it was the eye contact. I think I let it go on too long, and my brain started misinterpreting things. Attaching feelings to something simply because of the intensity of the moment.

*It didn't mean anything.*

I mean, this is Echo we're talking about. The same man who breaks into my apartment, watches me sleep, and says deeply deranged things so confidently that my brain forgets I'm supposed to be alarmed by them. Of course sex with him was intense. Of course the aftermath felt even more intense. Everything about him is intense. He doesn't know how to do anything casually, but that doesn't magically turn one hookup into some grand emotional revelation.

If anything, it just proves that we need to keep doing it.

The first time is always weird. It's loaded with so much curiosity and buildup that it makes everything feel bigger than it is. But if we keep hooking up, that'll take the novelty out of this. It'll prove that this thing between us is just chemistry and terrible judgment and a mutual inability to keep our hands off each other. It'll take the pressure off, so we can finally think clearly and see that this is nothing more than a friends with benefits situation.

I exhale slowly, feeling some of the knots in my stomach loosen.

*Yeah.* That's what we'll do. Next time, there will be no prolonged eye contact. No letting the moment linger so long that it grows feelings where there shouldn't be any. We'll have sex and act like normal adults about it.

I can control this. I *know* I can. I just need to treat it for what it is instead of letting my imagination run wild and turn a little post-sex intensity into something it's not.

I reach for my phone on the nightstand and open my text thread with Echo.

My thumb hovers over the keyboard as guilt gnaws at me. I should probably apologize for what happened. Or at the very least, acknowledge it. But the second I think about sending anything remotely sincere, my entire body recoils.

*No,* that would feed into the exact problem I'm trying to avoid.

I send him a different message. One that should make this feel simple again.

> See you tomorrow?

His reply comes through immediately.

> Of course

I set my phone back on the nightstand and pull the sheet up higher, ignoring the fact that my bed feels a little too empty without him in it.

# CHAPTER TWENTY

Brian the barista is flirting again.

I watch him from across the coffee shop, leaning over the counter with that goofy smile he probably thinks is charming. The woman he's currently hassling isn't Dahlia, but with the way he's trying to sweet-talk her, it might as well be. I've read enough of her texts with Fallon to know that this type of behavior is normal for him.

He's done it to both of them on more than a few occasions, and every time it's the same. Flirt with them aggressively at the register, then once their drinks are done, he holds them for ransom while he pesters them for their contact info. The girls never gave in to him, but the fact that he did it to them at all grates on my nerves. His job is to make them their fucking drinks, not to make them uncomfortable.

I step up to the counter and when Brian the barista sees me, his smile doesn't drop exactly, but it does recalibrate.

"Good morning, sir. What can I get you?"

I came here for two reasons.

The first is the drinks. Dahlia and Fallon have been

texting about them since seven this morning. I guess it's some seasonal drink launch today. One that they've been tracking like a national holiday. They were planning to pick up the drinks an hour from now. I decided to save them the trip.

The second reason is standing right in front of me with a dirty green apron on and a black marker clenched in his hand. Asshole has no idea what's coming for him.

"Two large iced chais with extra pumpkin cold foam."

He asks if there's anything else, and when I shake my head, he gives me my total. I pull out my wallet, unhurriedly, and pause.

"Actually, there is something else." I say, leveling my gaze at him as I lean in a little closer. "You wouldn't happen to know if any of your coworkers have gotten a little aggressive with some of the female customers recently?"

His eyes widen, then shift back and forth uncomfortably.

"My wife mentioned something about it a few weeks back." I continue, ignoring how good it feels to call her that. "She said whoever it was made her pretty uncomfortable." I tilt my head slightly.

Brian the barista has gone very still.

"She didn't give me a name though."

"I don't— I mean, not that I know of, sir." He says, eyeing me warily. His voice manages to come out even, but I can see the muscles working in his throat.

"Hm." I nod slowly, pretending as if I'm genuinely considering his words. "Well, if you hear anything, do me a favor and tell him to be more respectful." I hold his gaze. "I'd hate to have to come back and cause a scene because some asshole couldn't take a fucking hint."

He swallows and nods his head emphatically.

"Of course. Name for the cup?" He asks.

I flash him a smile. "It's for my wife and her friend." I

say, tasting the word on my tongue again. "Dahlia and Fallon."

I watch his face as recognition moves through it like a current. He uncaps his marker and scribbles their names on the cups without another word.

The girls' drinks are ready a few minutes later, and when he sets them on the counter, he refuses to look me in the eye.

I smile to myself as I reach for them.

*That should take care of that.*

WHEN I STEP THROUGH THE DOOR OF BETTER THAN FICTION, Fallon is the first to see me. She's perched on the counter, legs swinging, talking to Dahlia while she stocks her bestsellers shelf. Her eyes land on the drinks in my hands, and her face instantly brightens.

"No way." She says, shaking her head in disbelief. "Please tell me one of those is for me."

I give her a nod as I step closer and set the drinks on the counter beside her. "Even has your name on it." I say smoothly. "Anything to stay on your good side."

Bambi turns around to look at me, and when our eyes meet, instead of smiling, like I know she wants to, she bites the inside of her cheek and shakes her head.

"I see you've resorted to bribery." She quips, cocking a brow at me. "You know you can't just buy our friendship, right?"

Fallon reaches for her drink and takes a long sip. "Don't listen to her." She says, waving her hand dismissively. "I'm not above being bought."

Dahlia picks up her drink without looking at me, then pauses when she notices the contents.

"You brought us pumpkin cold foam chais? How did you know?"

"You mentioned it this morning."

I don't say the concerning part out loud. That it wasn't technically me she mentioned it to.

The look she gives me sits somewhere between outrage and resignation. She wants to be upset about the violation of her privacy, but I think by now she's learned that there's no boundary I won't cross to make her happy.

She takes a sip, and the smile that spreads across her face makes the corner of my mouth twitch.

*That. That alone right there made this trip worth it.*

"So..." Bambi drawls, setting her cup back down on the counter. "What are you doing here? You know, besides being our magical pumpkin chai fairy?"

"I need book two."

"You actually finished it?"

"I did."

Surprise briefly flickers across her face before she quickly smooths her features again.

"Finished what?" Fallon asks, eyes flicking between the two of us.

"Darkfever." Bambi says, tilting her head at me.

Fallon stifles a laugh. "D, you did not make him read faerie porn."

"I actually had no hand in it. Echo picked it out himself."

"Seriously?" Fallon asks, looking at me.

I nod, never taking my eyes off Bambi. "She said it was her favorite, and I had to know why."

Fallon clears her throat and hops off the counter. "I'm gonna go... do something else right now. You two have fun."

As soon as she's out of earshot, Bambi narrows her eyes at me. "You scared her off."

"That's okay." I say, licking my lips. "As long as I'm not doing the same to you."

She bites the inside of her cheek. "You should be," she says softly. "You read my texts, you spy on me, you sneak into my room every night. All of that should scare me."

I work the muscles in my jaw. "But does it?"

Bambi doesn't answer right away. I search her face, looking for anything that might give me insight into what she's thinking. I'm desperate for her answer in a way I've never been desperate for anything before.

"No."

The word lands quietly between us, and she holds my gaze.

"No." She says it again. "Which probably means my judgment is shit."

"Or it's more perceptive than you realize."

Her brow furrows, and her mouth moves, like she's on the precipice of saying something, then she pauses, clears her throat, and picks up her drink instead.

I don't push her, even though every instinct I have is begging me to. Pushing her would be stupid, and I'm trying very hard not to be stupid around her.

"So, book two, right?" She says, swiftly changing the subject.

"Book two." I agree, nodding my head.

Bambi moves through the stacks and comes back with the book in hand. She holds it out to me, and when I reach for it, my fingers graze against hers. She jolts at the contact and pulls her hand back before straightening her shoulders and pretending like it didn't happen.

This is who we are in the daylight. She keeps a barrier between us, calls me her friend, and acts like every small thing I do for her is mildly irritating. But at night the barrier's gone and so is the performance. She stops pretending she doesn't want me, because there's no one left to pretend for.

It's not enough. It'll never be enough, but it's what I have. And I'll take every version she's willing to give me.

"I'll see you tonight," I say, picking up the book and tucking it into the crook of my arm.

"Maybe." She says coyly, which is daytime Bambi's version of yes.

I turn to leave and catch Fallon watching us over the lid of her cup. She gives me a quiet, knowing look and raises her half-finished chai in a small toast.

I give her a nod and walk out the door.

Her best friend doesn't completely hate me. *That's good.* My future wife needs someone in her life who isn't trying to talk her out of this.

# CHAPTER TWENTY-ONE

DAHLIA

"Hey stranger." Fallon says, flashing me a smile as she steps through the front door of our apartment. "I feel like I haven't seen you in forever."

I look up from my phone and smile back at her. "I know, right? I don't know how we keep missing each other."

Fallon plops on the couch beside me and gives me a knowing look.

"What?"

"Nothing." She says innocently, stretching her long arms with a yawn. "So where's your boy?"

I narrow my eyes at her. "Who, Echo? How should I know?"

"I figured he's probably busy with something." She says, shrugging as she grabs an apple from the fruit bowl on our coffee table. "He's usually attached to your hip."

"No, he isn't." I insist, scowling at her. "That's ridiculous."

"Oh, he is." She says, leaning back into the couch with a

smirk. "You just don't notice because you like him being there. You might even actually like him."

"I do not like Echo," I grumble, but even I don't feel any conviction behind the words.

Fallon laughs. "Whatever you say, D."

I glare at her. "You're so annoying."

"But also kinda right, right?"

I want to argue. I want to list all the reasons she's wrong. But I can't think of a single one that doesn't sound like a lie. *Fucking hell.*

Seeing the frustration on my face, Fallon's smug expression softens. "It's not the end of the world if you do like him, you know."

"I know. But we're just friends."

*At least, that's what we're supposed to be.*

"Well, if your feelings ever change, just know he has my stamp of approval."

I frown. "Yeah, about that. Why do you like him? You usually don't like any of the guys I date."

Fallon takes a bite of her apple and responds mid-chew. "It's not that I don't like them. I just see through their bullshit."

"I get that. But how is Echo any different?"

Fallon sets her apple down and turns to face me.

"Honestly, I don't know." She says, her voice taking on a more serious tone. "His intentions just seem… good."

I eye her suspiciously. "You got that from talking to him for like five minutes total?"

"Nooo." She says, tilting her head. "People can easily feed you bullshit with their words, so I never trust what comes out of their mouth. I got that from the way he looks at you."

I wrinkle my nose. "Explain."

Fallon sighs and looks up, like she's trying to choose her next words carefully.

"Most men look at women they're attracted to and immediately start thinking about what they want to do to them." She says. "And if you pay attention, those thoughts are written all over their faces."

I nod my head and grab one of the throw pillows to start fidgeting with one of the tassels.

"When Echo looks at you, it's like he's thinking about what he could do *for* you. He watches you. He adjusts to what you need. And yeah, I know that sounds intense, but I think a part of you can sense that too."

My fingers still on the tassel, and I look up at her. "What makes you think that?"

"Because when you're around him, you don't hold back. You don't explain yourself. You don't apologize for existing like you've done with other guys you've dated. You just… let yourself be." She pauses. "You never do that with anyone. Not even me."

I work the muscles in my throat.

She's right. I don't explain myself to Echo. I never have. I don't apologize for being sharp or guarded or too much. I just… am. And he never asks me to be anything else.

"Not to mention." Fallon continues. "You're literally never home anymore. Haven't you noticed you spend almost every day with him now?"

I open my mouth to deny it, but I can't. I do spend most of my days with him now. It's never planned. It just happens.

Echo shows up at the bookstore with coffee. Or texts asking if I'm hungry. Or mentions he's nearby and thought he'd stop by. And somehow, by the end of the night, we're together. Talking. Or not talking. Just existing in the same space. And I don't mind it. In fact, I kind of look forward to it.

*Shit.*

When did this happen?

When did I start letting him in?

When did I stop seeing him as the man from the alley and start seeing him as... this?

*Fuck.*

I can't let myself get attached. Attachment leads to expectations. Expectations lead to love. Love leads to disaster. And I can't survive another one of those.

My phone buzzes on the couch beside me. I pick it up and glance at the screen. Echo texted me.

> You eat yet?

I stare at the message. Three simple words. Nothing demanding. Nothing possessive. Nothing even remotely concerning. He's just checking in on me like he always does.

*So why does it feel so suffocating?*

I scroll up through our thread. Past today's message. Past yesterday's. Past the weeks of constant back-and-forth that I didn't even notice piling up.

*When did this become my routine?*

*When did he become such a big part of my world?*

"I didn't realize." I say numbly. "It kind of just happened."

"Stop freaking out." Fallon says, studying my face. "Echo is a good guy, don't overthink this."

That's precisely the problem. Echo *isn't* a good guy. He's a bad guy, and he's never pretended to be anything else.

I know what he's capable of. I've witnessed it firsthand,

and the last thing I should be doing is catching feelings for him. If anything, I should be actively avoiding him.

Under the guise of friendship, what was happening between us felt safe, and that label made it easy for me to let my guard down. But now, I'm wondering if that was a mistake.

My phone buzzes with another incoming message, and my eyes snap to the screen. Josh texted me.

> Hey, Doll. Just checking in since I haven't
> heard from you. How are you?

I stare at the message and roll my eyes at the ironic timing.

*Fucking awful, Josh, but thanks for asking. You haven't heard from me partially because I'm too much of a coward to give you an explanation, and partially because I think you might love me. Which won't work because the last person who loved me murdered my whole family. And to make matters worse, I think I'm catching feelings for someone even more dangerous than him. So yeah, I'm not doing great.*

I set my phone down on the couch and press my palms against my eyes.

I'm such an asshole. I should've given Josh closure weeks ago. I told him I'd reach out, but every time I tried to force myself to reach out and rip the fucking band-aid off, my brain just... slid away from it. Like it was jerking back from touching a hot stove. It's been easier to think about Echo. Safer, in a weird way, even though he's way more dangerous.

I open Josh's text thread and start typing.

> Hey. Sorry, I've been MIA. Do you want to
> go grab coffee and talk? I'm free today.

My thumb hovers over the send button. This is stupid. I

know it's stupid. I shouldn't text Josh back. It's just asking for trouble. Then again, Echo doesn't own me, and I don't need his permission to talk to anyone. We're just friends.

My phone buzzes again with a text from Echo.

> Have dinner with me. There's a new Thai place downtown.

My heart flutters like the traitorous little bitch it is, and I inwardly curse at myself.

*What the hell is wrong with me?*

The lines are blurring between us and I'm starting to feel things I shouldn't. Things that I've purposely shielded myself from feeling for the last decade.

I hit send on the message to Josh before I can change my mind. His reply comes almost immediately.

> Let's do dinner instead. Pick you up at 6?

I swallow hard.

> Sounds good.

I set my phone face-down on the couch and sigh. When I look up, Fallon is watching me.

"What?" I ask, more defensively than I mean to.

"Nothing." She replies, but there's judgement in her tone. I can feel it. "Who was that?"

"Josh." I say, averting my gaze. "We're going to grab dinner tonight. It's not a big deal."

"I didn't say it was."

I look up at her, and the way she's looking at me says she knows exactly what I'm doing. And why.

"Just be careful." Fallon says, looking down at her phone. "Feelings aren't something to ignore."

"I'm not ignoring my feelings."

She glances up at me. "I wasn't talking about yours."

# CHAPTER TWENTY-TWO

DAHLIA

THE RESTAURANT JOSH PICKED SCREAMS EFFORT.

Crisp white tablecloths, crystal chandeliers, and a wine list so extensive it requires a sommelier. It's nice. Too nice.

I shift in my seat and tug at the hem of my dress. I shouldn't have worn this. The soft yellow color reminds me of Echo, and it makes this whole situation feel like even more of a betrayal.

I shouldn't have agreed to go to dinner either. It was supposed to be coffee. Coffee is chill, casual. A dinner at a place like this is anything but. If I'm being real, I shouldn't have texted Josh at all, but I'm here now, so I'll just have to get through it.

Josh is talking again. Just like he has been for the last twenty minutes. He's been going on and on about his job and the recent promotion he accepted.

I nod at the right times. Smile when it seems appropriate. And keep my eyes locked on the fine lines in his forehead to feign eye contact. But the whole time, I'm thinking about how wrong this feels. How stiff I am. How forced my responses sound. And how I keep checking my phone under the table even though I know I haven't gotten any new messages.

Fallon's words circle in my head.

*Most men look at women and think about what they want to do to them. Echo looks at you like he's thinking about what he could do for you.*

I glance at Josh. He's leaning forward slightly, his wine glass held loosely in one hand. He's looking at me like he's already planned our next five dates. Like this is just the beginning of something he's decided we're going to be. And I feel nothing. No spark. No comfort. No ease. Just stiffness.

"What do you think, Doll?"

I blink and refocus on him. "Sorry, what?"

Josh gives me a patient smile. "I asked if you wanted to split the pappardelle."

"Oh. Sure. Yeah."

He signals the waiter over, and I take a sip of water, trying to steady myself.

This was a mistake. I just need to get through dinner, go home, and never talk to him again.

I'm debating whether I should make an excuse to leave early when movement near the front door catches my eye.

Echo's here and my stomach drops so fast it feels like I'm going to be sick.

*Fuck.*

He stops just inside the entrance, scanning the restaurant, cataloging every exit, every face, every potential threat. Then his eyes find mine. And they're cold.

Not the controlled calm I'm used to. Not the careful neutrality he wears like armor. Cold. Hard. Lethal.

My eyes widen, and I open my mouth, desperate to say

something that'll get me up from this table before Echo reaches it. But my brain stalls, and he's already moving.

Echo cuts through the dining room with long, purposeful strides that make the space feel smaller. People glance up as he passes. A waiter steps aside instinctively. Even the indistinct murmur of conversation seems to dip as he approaches.

Echo doesn't just walk into a room. He fills it. And right now, standing at the edge of our table, he seems to tower over everything. Over Josh. Over the chandelier above us. Over the whole fucking restaurant. I have to tilt my head back just to meet his gaze.

He's wearing his dark coat, the one that makes his shoulders look even broader. His jaw is tight. His hands are still tucked into his pockets, but there's tension radiating off him in waves. He looks like he's holding himself back from doing something violent.

I study his face for a beat, searching for something. Softness, hesitation, anything that tells me he's not about to cause a scene. But there's nothing. Just that cold, controlled fury I've only seen once before. In the alley.

My chest tightens with a confusing tangle of relief and dread. Relief, because the part of me that craves his presence is happy to see him. And dread, because I know he's not here just to talk.

"Bambi," he says quietly. "Let's go."

Josh's eyes ping-pong between me and Echo.

"What are you doing here?" I ask, my voice barely above a whisper.

Echo exhales and levels Josh with an icy glare.

"Getting you away from him."

Josh flinches, his polite smile faltering. "I'm sorry?"

Echo ignores him and sets his gaze on me.

"He's dangerous, Bambi."

Josh laughs once and swallows. "What are you talking about?"

"He googled you." Echo says, clenching his jaw. "Before you started seeing each other, he knew everything about you."

Echo's words land like a bomb, and silence crashes over the table. I can hear the low rumblings of conversation from the tables around us. The soft clinking of silverware against porcelain. But at our table, there's nothing but complete and utter silence.

Echo doesn't repeat himself. He just stands there staring Josh down like he's waiting for him to crack.

"What?" Josh shakes his head and gives Echo a tight-lipped smile. "Are you serious? Everyone googles people before they go out with them."

I chew on my lip. He's right. Everyone does that. I did it too, before Josh and I started dating.

"You didn't just look up her social media," Echo sneers. "You dug into everything about her." He pauses, letting the words settle. "Multiple times."

Josh looks at me, and his smile tightens at the edges as his jaw flexes. "Doll, that's normal, right?"

I glare at Josh and find myself at a loss for words. If he did try to dig into my past, he wouldn't have found anything. I changed my name ten years ago and barely have an online presence now.

*Still, that isn't normal. It's weird.*

"He did it weeks before he even had your number," Echo adds, curling his lip. "There's nothing normal about that."

Josh's soft expression falters, just for a second, before he quickly forces it back on. He leans back in his chair and rubs the back of his neck.

"Look, I saw you in the bookstore before we met," he

says, keeping his voice light. "I didn't know how to talk to you. So yeah, I looked you up, and I probably took it too far." He glances at me, his eyes soft. "I just wanted to be prepared for when I worked up the nerve to talk to you."

His excuse is plausible. Expected even, given what I know about him. He's exactly the kind of man who would want to be fully prepared before he approached me. *Still.* That doesn't make it okay. Not by a long shot.

"He's a liar, Bambi," Echo says flatly. "You can't trust him."

I look up at Echo, and something in me snaps. Not because anything he's saying is wrong. In fact, I'm sure he's right, but the thing is, he shouldn't be.

He shouldn't know Josh's search history. He shouldn't know what he looked up or when or how many fucking times he did it. But he does, and chances are, he's been monitoring my search history too. Digging into my life. Into the people I talk to. Into the choices I make. Without asking. Without permission.

The realization slaps me in the face.

Echo didn't just happen to run into us. He's been watching. Cataloging. Collecting data on every person who gets close to me, treating me like I'm something he needs to manage. And what's worse is he doesn't even see a problem with it.

He's standing there, jaw tight, eyes cold, fully convinced he's protecting me. That this is what I need. What I deserve. But all I can think is that he's doing the same thing Josh did. The same thing Christian did all those years ago.

Making decisions for me. Crossing boundaries he has no right to cross. The only difference is Echo is better at hiding his tracks.

I stand up abruptly, my chair scraping loudly against the floor.

"Echo, can we talk?" I ask, my voice shaking, as I lock my eyes on his. "Alone?"

He glances at Josh, his eyes narrowing slightly, like he's debating whether or not he could get away with snapping his neck in a restaurant full of witnesses. Then he gives me a stiff nod and steps back from the table.

I follow him toward the entrance, and the second we're out of earshot from everyone else, I turn to face him.

"What the hell are you doing?" I hiss.

"Keeping you safe."

"From what? A dinner date?"

"From him." He replies through clenched teeth. "Bambi, I know you don't want to hear this, but Josh is dangerous."

"And how did you figure that out?" I ask, crossing my arms. "Did you run a background check? Hack into his computer? What?"

Echo presses his lips together.

"Did you do the same thing to me?" I ask softly. "Is that —is that how you knew where to find me?"

He doesn't answer, which is answer enough.

"Oh, my fucking god." I say, pressing my fingers to my temples as every coincidence that wasn't a coincidence runs through my head. "You have been, haven't you?"

"Bambi—"

"No." I drop my hands and look at him. At the hard line of his mouth. At the tension radiating off him in waves. At the way he's crowding me, like he's trying to physically block me from going back to the table. "You don't get to do this. You don't get to dig into people's lives without asking. You don't get to show up and make decisions for me."

"I'm trying to protect you."

"I never asked you to protect me!"

Echo goes still. Completely, utterly still.

For a moment, neither of us says anything. I can hear my own breathing. Can feel the heat creeping up my neck, and the sting of tears I refuse to let fall.

"Look. I hear you," I say finally, forcing my voice to steady. "I get it, and I believe you. I know you think you're helping. But this is my problem to handle. Not yours." I swallow hard, my throat tight. "So please, just go."

"I'm not leaving you with him."

"Echo, I swear to God, if you don't stop, I will never ever speak to you again. Is that what you want?"

Echo stares at me. And I see the exact moment my words hit him. Hurt flashes across his face, and his jaw clenches so hard I'm afraid his teeth might crack. Then, without saying another word, he turns and walks out.

The door swings shut behind him, and I immediately want to take back everything that just happened. Every word. Every accusation. Every single thing that made the one person I can be myself with, look at me like that.

Even though it hurts, I force myself to turn around. And after taking a second to clear my head, I walk back to the table on legs that don't quite feel like my own.

Josh watches me approach, and the smugness in his expression makes my stomach churn. He literally looks like he just won something, which pisses me off because what just happened had nothing to do with him.

"That was intense," Josh says, smiling at me as I take my seat across from him.

"Yeah." I reply, placing the napkin on my lap without really looking at him. "It was."

He leans forward. "What the hell was his problem, anyway?"

I glare at him.

Is he really going to blame this all on Echo? I mean, sure, Echo's tactics completely crossed the line, but nothing he said was untrue. It is weird that Josh looked into my past before he met me, and for him to not even apologize or at the very least acknowledge that what he did was wrong is crazy.

*Fuck this.* I don't even want to be here. And it's not like I plan on seeing him again after this, so what's the point of forcing myself to sit through this dinner?

"Actually," I say, grabbing my purse as I stand up from the table. "I'm gonna go."

Josh cocks his head. "What? We haven't even eaten yet."

"I know. But this isn't going anywhere, and it's not fair for me to pretend like it is."

"Dahlia, wait—" He says, reaching for my hand, but I manage to pull back before he can touch me.

"Don't," I say firmly.

His expression hardens. "You're serious."

"Yes."

"Because of him?"

"Because of me." I take a step back. "And because of what you did. Regardless of your intentions, digging into my past like that was wrong, Josh. I'm done. We're done."

I turn and walk out before he can say anything else.

The second I'm outside, I stop and pull out my phone. No new messages. I stare at the screen, waiting for some kind of sign from Echo that I know isn't coming. He's gone. And I'm the one who told him to go.

I lock my phone and slip it back into my purse, knowing that for the first time in weeks, I'm completely on my own. No one watching. No one following. No one making deci-sions for me.

This is what I wanted.

So why does it feel like I just made a huge mistake?

# CHAPTER TWENTY-THREE

*Echo*

THE WAREHOUSE WE OWN IN THE MISSION DISTRICT IS DARK when I arrive. To anyone passing by, it would look completely abandoned, but that's precisely the point.

River texted an hour ago letting me know that Mikey, one of our low-level dealers, tried to skim product off one of our shipments. He thought he was smart enough to hide it. He wasn't.

I find him in the back room, tied to a chair, and bleeding from his swollen left eye.

"He's all yours." Briggs says, stepping aside.

I give him a smirk as I roll up my sleeves and crack my neck.

Inflicting pain is what I'm good at, what I fucking excel at. I don't hesitate. I don't second-guess. And I have zero confusion about what my role is in this domain. This is the one part of my job where I thrive.

Mikey's eyes widen when he sees me, recognition clicking automatically. He knows who I am and what I do for this family. He should be scared. He should be petrified.

"I'm going to ask you some questions." I say, circling him slowly. "You're going to answer them. If you lie, I'll know. If you stall, I'll know. And if you waste my fucking time—" I pause, letting the sentence hang. "Then I'll make it hurt more. Understand?"

He nods frantically.

"First question, who helped you?"

Panic morphs the lines of his face, and his eyes widen in disbelief.

In this organization, stealing from us is a death sentence, and every single person on our payroll knows it. Mikey is no fucking leader, so someone else had to have convinced him this shit was worth dying for.

"N-no one. Just me. I swear—"

*Lie.*

The amount of product missing alone would've required more than one person to move. Not to mention, we never let anyone near the shipments alone. Someone had to help him, or at the very least turn a blind eye.

I smash my fist into the side of face with lethal precision, relishing in the feel of my knuckles breaking skin.

"Try again." I hiss, glaring at him.

"Fuck!" He wails, choking on the blood gushing through his teeth. "I-It was just me. I—"

I smash my fist into his face again, harder this time, and his head whips to the side unnaturally. Blood sprays from his mouth and splatters on the concrete floor. Mikey looks up at me pathetically, probably expecting me to feel a semblance of sympathy for him, but I don't feel anything other than the calculated ruthlessness I was trained to feel.

That's the thing people don't understand about me. This part, the part where I'm in a room like this with a purpose and a clear set of instructions, is the only place where everything gets quiet. I'm useful here. I'm good at this. And being good at something is the closest thing to peace I've ever known.

Bambi's voice cuts through my focus.

*What the hell are you doing?*

I blink and shake my head.

Mikey is talking now. Saying something, but I don't catch it.

"What?" I snap.

"I said there were two others." He gasps, half whine, half cry. "Arty a—and Jon. Arty helped me move product, while Jon stood watch."

"Where is it now?"

"SafetyStorage off I-5 in Downey. Unit 47."

I pull out my phone to text River the location. It takes me a few tries because my hands are shaking.

*Why the fuck are my hands shaking?*

I stare at them like they've betrayed me. They don't shake. They never fucking shake. Not in rooms like this. Not when I'm doing the one thing I've always been certain of.

"How much did you take?" I ask, refocusing.

"Fifty. Maybe sixty. I don't know—"

"Sixty kilos of cocaine and you thought no one would notice?"

"I was gonna put it back! I just needed time—"

Before he can finish, my fists are colliding with his face in rapid succession. My knuckles split under the pressure, but I don't let up. I need the release just as much as he needs the message.

I hit him once, twice, three times, then lose count somewhere around the seventh hit.

Bambi's voice infiltrates my brain again.

*I never asked you to protect me!*

"Echo." Briggs calls from somewhere behind me, but I don't turn around.

"Answer the question, motherfucker." I shout.

The man's crying now, but I don't let up. *I can't.* I need to finish this. I need to stay focused. But all I can see is Bambi's face.

"Echo." Briggs calls again. Firmer this time.

I turn and glare at him.

"What?"

"You didn't ask him a question."

I look back at the man. His teeth are all shattered, and his face is a bloody mess, but he's still breathing, barely.

*Fuck.*

"I need a minute," I mutter, heading for the door.

"Where are you going?"

"I said I need a fucking minute."

"We're not done—"

"I am. You finish it."

I'm outside before Briggs can respond.

The air outside is cold, but it does nothing to distract me from the mess in my head. I take a seat on the curb and pull out my phone, and open the tracker. Bambi is home. She has been for the last forty minutes. *She's safe.*

I close the app. Then I open it again and close it one more time.

*What the fuck am I doing?*

I lean against the wall and press the heels of my palms into my eyes. The worst part isn't that I lost focus. The worst part is that I know exactly why I did.

In every room that's ever mattered to me, I've had a role. A function. Something I was designed for that made my presence make sense. In my world, I'm the weapon.

But out there, in the real world with Bambi, I don't know

what the fuck I am anymore. She made it clear she doesn't want my help, but I don't know what to be if I can't be of service. Protecting others is the only thing I've ever been good at.

The door opens behind me, and Briggs takes a seat on the curb beside me. He pulls out a pack of cigarettes and lights one up, and hands it to me before pulling out another and lighting his own.

"He got loose." He says calmly, blowing out a puff of smoke.

I flick off the ash and snap my head towards him. "What?"

"Mikey. You accidentally loosened his restraints. He got free and tried to make a run for it. I caught him. Barely, but —" He pauses, studying my face. "Where the fuck is your head at?"

*On her. On the way she looked at me like I disgusted her.*

"This isn't you." Briggs continues. "You don't make mistakes. You don't lose focus. What's going on?"

"Nothing."

"Bullshit." He says, lifting his head to look at the night sky. "We've been best friends since we were kids, asshole. I can tell something's going on with you."

I meet his eyes. "It's handled."

"Clearly, it's not."

He's right. I know he's right.

"I'll take care of it," I say, taking another inhale.

"How?"

I don't give him an answer. Partly because I don't want him getting more involved in this than he already is, and partly because I don't have one for him.

"Is this about a girl?"

When I don't answer right away, he exhales sharply and shakes his head. "Jesus, Echo. You're smarter than this."

"I know."

"Then act like it."

He takes one last puff of his cigarette, stubs it out on the sidewalk, then stands to his full height. "I'll finish up here. You go home and get your head straight."

I stay outside for another few minutes, staring at the sky and thinking about what to do next. Then I pull out my phone and open her tracker one last time.

*Still home. Still safe.*

When it comes to securing her safety, I know exactly what to do. Break hands. Remove threats. End problems. That part is easy. Getting her to accept me? To admit what this really is? That's something else entirely.

Every instinct I have is telling me to keep pressing. To close the distance. To back her into a corner until she can't pretend this isn't happening. And it's getting harder to fight against those urges.

She got in my head tonight, and because of that, I lost control and nearly fucked everything up. I can't keep obsessing over her like this, and I'm sick of being at her mercy.

*Bambi wants me to stop?* Fine. I will.

I'll step back. I'll go quiet. And we'll see how long she keeps wanting to stay "friends" when I'm not there to blur the lines for her anymore.

# CHAPTER TWENTY-FOUR

DAHLIA

Rain trickles down the front windows of the bookstore in streams, blurring the world outside into nothing more than smears of headlights and slick asphalt. The sun set a few hours ago, taking its warmth with it, and another soul hasn't set foot in Better Than Fiction since.

I should just close early. If it were any other day, I would. But Fallon is working the night shift tonight, and the thought of coming home to an empty loft even earlier than planned just doesn't sound appealing.

I miss Mom and Dad extra tonight. If they were still around, I could just head over to their place for the night. I'd gorge myself on Dad's food and binge-watch my favorite Filipino soap operas with Mom. Instead, I'm stuck here. Alone.

Echo hasn't contacted me in over two weeks. Which is fine. I told him to stop, and he did. But I think I just got too used to him being there. The constant texts. The random check-ins. The way he always seemed to know what I was thinking.

Echo took up space in my world. And now that he's gone, I feel his absence. And I really hate that I do.

It's just so unlike him to disappear like this.

I slip my phone out of my pocket and quickly check the notifications. No new messages. *Damn.*

He's always been vague about his work, but judging by how effortlessly he killed those men in the alley, I know he isn't sitting at a desk for a living.

*Maybe something happened to him.* I swallow hard. *God, I really hope nothing bad happened to him.*

I restart my phone and wait for it to power back on. Maybe my connection is off. Or there's some kind of network error. Nothing again. I lock the screen and slip it back into my pocket, feeling embarrassed for even bothering.

*God Dahlia, get a grip on yourself. This is what you wanted.*

The rain picks up outside, tapping harder against the windows. My shoulders tighten before I can stop them. I move behind the counter and start straightening things that don't need to be straightened. A stack of bookmarks. A cup filled with pens. The little chalkboard sign with our book of the week. Anything to keep my mind distracted and my hands busy.

I'm adjusting a crooked pile of paperbacks when my phone buzzes. The sound ricochets through the store, and my heart jumps so hard it almost hurts. I grab it without thinking and answer it.

"Dahlia Nocon?" A man on the other end asks, his voice professional and familiar in the worst possible way.

My stomach drops. I haven't heard anyone call me by my real last name in years. "Yes." I manage. "This is her."

"This is Detective Harris with the Franklin County Sheriff's Department's Major Crimes Unit."

He pauses, and in that silence, I know something is wrong. I sit down slowly on the stool behind the counter. "I wanted to inform you personally before the news goes public. Christian Sanders escaped custody two nights ago."

I try to process what he's saying, but his words don't make sense. They can't make sense.

"I'm sorry, what?" I ask, my voice strangled, barely audible.

He clears his throat. "There was an incident while he was being transferred to another facility. We're-"

"How?" I interrupt. "How did this happen? He was supposed to be locked up. He was supposed to-"

"We're still investigating the details, but I wanted you to be aware. He hasn't contacted any of his immediate family, so we have reason to believe that he may attempt to contact you. I understand this is alarming, but—"

The rest of his words fade as my phone slips from my fingers and hits the rug with a dull thud.

**Christian is out.**

The room tilts and I grab onto the edge of the counter to steady myself.

*This can't be happening.*

*This can't be fucking happening.*

I worked so hard to escape my past. I changed my last name, moved across the country, and built a whole new life for myself. And now, the safe little life I've made for myself is at risk. All because they let him slip through their fingers.

I slip off the stool and slide down to the floor, pressing my back against a bookshelf as I pull my knees to my chest.

*What if he comes for me?*

*What if he finds me?*

*What if—*

Fuck, I need to calm down. My heart is beating so hard, it

feels like it's trying to leap out of my chest, and every ragged breath I pull in feels harder than the last, like the air is too thick for my lungs to take in. I claw at my neck and try to ground myself by taking slow and steady breaths, but it's no use. My mind won't stop racing.

Lightning strikes, and a second later thunder rattles the windows, making my head snap up instinctively. A wall of rain-streaked windows stares back at me, and I've never felt more exposed in my life.

I race to lock the door, flip the open sign to closed, and then pull the curtains shut over the front windows, sealing myself off from the street. I retreat to the back room and close the door, pressing my forehead against the cool wall as I try to breathe through the panic blooming in my chest.

I pull my phone out again, and my thumb hovers over Fallon's name, but I hesitate. She's working and telling her now will only make her worry.

Then I glance at Echo's name, and without thinking, I call him. It takes a second for my brain to catch up, and when it does, I quickly end the call before the second ring.

*Calm down.* I think to myself. *You're not thinking clearly.*

I slide down the wall and sit on the floor, folding in on myself, and breathing slowly with my head between my knees like I've done a hundred times before.

My phone vibrates in my hand, but I can't bring myself to look at it right now. I don't want any more bad news, and I don't want anyone to hear me like this.

Eventually, the vibrations stop, and the silence that follows is deafening, but I allow myself to wallow in it and cry.

Once I'm finally able to breathe again, I wipe my face with the back of my sleeve and force myself to stand.

I can't hide back here forever.

I step back into the store, and the first thing my puffy eyes see when I glance at the front door, is the tall man standing outside of it.

*Echo is here.*

He's standing there, completely soaked, with rain streaming down his face and splattering against his dark gray suit. He's standing perfectly still beneath the torn awning, staring at me.

He could've knocked or forced his way in. But he didn't. He just *waited for me.*

Our eyes meet through the glass, and something inside me breaks open.

I cross the distance in three long strides, but as soon as I get there, I feel myself freeze.

If I let him in, if let him see me like this, with my walls fully demolished by ghosts of my past, there's no going back to how we were before. He'll see every vulnerable part of me, and I won't be strong enough to hide it.

The rain drums against the glass between us as I look up with my hand hovering inches from the lock, debating what to do.

For his part, Echo doesn't ask me to open it. He doesn't even imply that I should. He just watches me with those amber eyes of his that see way too much, and I realize, without a doubt, what I want to do.

Cold, damp air rushes inside as I open the door, carrying the smell of rain and asphalt and him. Echo steps just close enough that I can see the water clinging to his lashes, the darkened fabric of his suit jacket, and the way the muscles in his throat are working.

"What are you doing here?"

"You called me."

I swallow hard, my throat burning. "I didn't mean to."
He nods his head in quiet understanding. "I know."

# CHAPTER TWENTY-FIVE

ECHO

BAMBI DOESN'T ARGUE WHEN I TELL HER I'M TAKING HER home. That's how I know something is wrong. She follows me out into the rain without protest, moving stiffly as if each step requires conscious effort.

I stay close enough to intervene, but I don't touch her. My hand hovers just behind her back. She drifts into the space between us. Not leaning on me exactly, but staying close as if she needs something solid nearby.

Her hands are shaking. Not violently and not enough that anyone else would notice, but just enough that I do.

I open the passenger door for her and wait. She hesitates for a moment, her fingers tightening around the strap of her bag, then she slides into the seat and stares straight ahead. I shut the door gently and move around to the driver's side.

When I get in, I take a moment to look at her before I start the engine. It's the first time I've seen her like this. Unguarded. Soft. Still. This is the version she keeps to herself, the one stripped of all her defenses. Bambi in her rawest form.

She's always been pretty, but right now, her beauty has nothing to do with effort or awareness, and everything to do with who she is. The honesty of it is unsettling.

The drive to her apartment is silent, and the only sound flowing through the car is the windshield wipers squeaking across the glass. I keep my eyes on the road, but my awareness never drifts from her. I register everything about her without even trying to. The way her hands are folded tightly in her lap. The way her knee bounces before she notices and forces it still. The way she keeps swallowing like her emotions are clogging up her throat.

"You okay?" I ask, chancing a glance at her.

She gives me a stiff nod, without looking back at me, and keeps her eyes locked on the road. I don't believe her, not even for a second, but that doesn't feel like it matters right now.

Every question I've asked her since we met was designed to get closer to her without pushing. To map her gently. To learn the shape of all her defenses. But none of those questions could have prepared me for this.

Our building comes into view sooner than I expect, and I pull into my usual spot in the garage and turn off my engine. The sudden quiet presses around us, and as I step out and cross over to her side of the car, I wonder if she's noticed that I'm parked in my unit's assigned spot.

"Come on," I say quietly, opening her door. "I'll walk you up."

She nods and lets me help her out of the car.

Her balance is off as we walk to the elevator and ride it up to her floor. She fumbles with her keys, then stops and squeezes her eyes shut, like the process has suddenly become too much for her to handle. I gently take them from her and unlock it.

She steps inside and slips her shoes off at the door, while I stay at the threshold, already preparing to leave. I know it's time. This is the point where I give her space and don't let this turn into something she didn't ask for. Then I feel her hand close around my wrist.

Her hold is hesitant and soft, and she glares at her own hand like she's not even sure how it got there.

"Do you want me to come in, Bambi?"

She nods and finally looks up at me as her hand slips away.

I kick off my shoes, shuck off my suit jacket, and follow her inside.

Bambi's living room is exactly what I expected it to be. It's warm. Lived-in. And smells faintly of paperback books and vanilla florals. I've seen the living space layout before. It's the same standard floor plan as mine, but it's my first time seeing how she fills it.

She drops onto the couch, pulls her legs up, and stares into nothing as a shiver runs through her. Hating how cold she looks, I grab the blanket and drape it over her shoulders, then crouch near the fireplace and turn it on. The gas ignites with a low rush, flames catching and settling into a steady glow.

"I'll make you some tea."

I move through her kitchen quietly, heating the kettle, finding a box of chamomile, and grabbing two mugs from a cabinet. It feels strange being here like this, doing something so small and ordinary for her.

Once I'm done, I take a seat across from her and hand her a mug. She looks at me then, really looks, and takes a slow sip.

"You want to talk about it?" I ask.

She shakes her head.

"Okay."

We sit there in silence while the fire crackles softly in the fireplace. She stares into it, her expression distant and unfocused.

I hate that I don't know how to fix this. I can't threaten it. I can't remove it. I can't negotiate with it until it breaks. All I can do is be here for her.

I watch her for a while, taking in the way her shoulders slowly relax as the heat settles in, and the way her breathing evens out inch by inch. Eventually, her head tips, resting against the arm of the couch, and she falls asleep without realizing it.

I should go. That's what makes sense, and it's what I've done every other time when she's needed me to. I leave before she regrets it, before she can take it back, before she remembers she's supposed to be afraid of me.

Every other time we've interacted, it's been because I made it happen. I pushed for a response, or a reaction, or a fucking ounce of acknowledgement.

But this time, she gave it to me willingly. She called me. She grabbed my wrist. And, even though I'm sure the circumstances of why she's even allowing this right now are fucked, she wanted me here.

So I stay where I am, even though it goes against every instinct I have. Even though I already know how this ends. Tomorrow morning will come, and she'll pull back. She'll pretend this didn't happen, and she'll put distance between us like she always does.

But tonight, I'm here.

And that's all that fucking matters.

# CHAPTER TWENTY-SIX

DAHLIA

I WAKE UP WITH MY EYES CLOSED. FOR A FEW PRECIOUS seconds, nothing happens. Everything is fine, my past hasn't clawed its way back into the present, and my mind hovers in that quiet space between sleep and consciousness.

I cling to that feeling, hoping it might stay. Then my brain comes back online and the events of last night trickle in.

*Christian is out.*

Panic settles deep in my gut, just as it did last night, but thankfully, the tears don't follow.

*Breathe. You're okay.*

I keep my eyes closed and try to ground myself by slowly taking in every sensation. The feel of the soft couch beneath me. The puffiness of my eyes. The ache in my shoulders that never seems to go away.

*The presence of someone else.*

My eyes snap open and I find Echo asleep on the couch across from me. He's lying on his back with one arm tucked behind his head and the other draped across his stomach. His face is relaxed in a way I've never seen before, and his breathing is deep enough that I know he's really out.

He stayed the night.

I never let anyone stay the night. It's not a hard set rule or anything. It's just something I don't do.

Nights are easy to compartmentalize. Mornings aren't. Mornings come with expectations and conversations that assume continuity. There's something about the daylight that makes things feel way more intimate.

I scan the space around us, taking it all in. The blanket draped over me. The empty mugs on the coffee table. The faint imprint his boots left on the doormat before he kicked them off. All proof that this isn't a dream.

I sit there for another minute, letting the reality of the situation sink in.

There's a killer sleeping on my couch. The same killer who's been openly stalking me and has crossed countless boundaries since the night we met. The same killer I've been stupidly hooking up with, despite knowing all of that.

In my space. In my *home*. So why the hell is my heart pounding for an entirely different reason?

I look at Echo, unabashedly, and study everything about him. His long dark lashes fanning across his cheeks. His full brows framing his face perfectly. The way his lips downturn slightly, even while sleeping, like he's been sad his whole life. He looks younger like this. Less guarded. Almost peaceful.

I mindlessly wonder if anyone else has ever seen him this way.

I know what he's capable of. I've seen it firsthand. And yet, when I look at him, I don't see a monster. I see a man, a beautiful one at that, both inside and out. And I don't know what that says about me.

*This is ridiculous.*

Whatever my brain is doing right now needs to fucking stop.

I slide one foot off the couch, then the other, and carefully rise from the couch. The cushion creaks under my weight, and I wince.

"Bambi." He calls out, his voice slow and sleepy.

I freeze.

*Shit.* Of course, he heard me. I don't know why I thought I could slip away unnoticed when he seems incapable of missing anything, especially when it involves me.

I turn around to find Echo propped up on one elbow, rubbing his eyes like he's trying to orient himself to the room. His hair is a mess, flattened on one side, and there's a faint crease between his brows.

"Sorry," I say quietly. "I didn't mean to wake you."

"Don't worry about it."

I glance down at the floor, suddenly very aware of how close this moment is to becoming something I don't know how to navigate. My teeth sink into my lower lip.

He watches me for a minute, then asks. "You okay?"

It's a simple question. There's no pressure behind it or expectation, but it still catches me off guard.

"I'm fine," I say automatically.

It's not a lie. It's just not the full truth. I'm very far from okay, but not for the reasons he's probably thinking.

If he senses the deception, he doesn't call me on it. Instead, he shifts and sits up a little straighter.

"I should head out." He says.

There it is. The out. Relief should follow. That's usually how this goes. Someone offers distance. I take it gratefully and wrap it around myself like armor. Except... I don't want that from him.

I look up at him before I can catch myself. "Oh," I say, clearing my throat.

Echo's gaze flicks to my face, then away again. I can tell he's purposely not trying to add pressure to the moment.

"You had a rough night." He adds. "You probably want some privacy."

I nod because that makes sense. Because it's reasonable. Because he's handling this with more care than I expected him to.

"Are you hungry?" I ask suddenly.

The words come out louder than I intend, and I inwardly cringe at myself.

Echo looks at me.

"There's a cafe down the block," I continue. "I was going to go anyway."

I shrug, trying to act nonchalant. "You could come with. If you want."

I brace for him to question me. To poke and prod until he understands exactly what I'm thinking. Surprisingly enough, he doesn't.

"Okay." He says, giving me a nod.

Some of the awkwardness dissipates and the tightness in my chest loosens.

I grab my hoodie from the back of a barstool and pull it on, suddenly grateful for something to do with my hands. Echo stands too, moving easily through my space.

As we head for the door, I catch a glimpse of us reflected in the hallway mirror. Me, still puffy-eyed and rumpled. Him, dark and solid and entirely too pretty in the morning light.

Christian is still out there.

Nothing about that has changed.

But I don't feel like I need to crawl into a hole and hide. And I think I have Echo to thank for that.

Patty's on 5th is aggressively cheerful for this hour of the morning. Mint-green booths line the floor in neat rows, their vinyl seats gleaming under overhead lights that feel just a little too bright for how exhausted I am. Every table has its own mini-jukebox perched on it with chrome edges dulled from years of use. The walls are crowded with a mix of retro signs and framed ads that promise milkshakes, burgers, and happiness in equal measure.

Echo holds the door open for me, and as I slip past him, my shoulder brushes his chest. It's impossible not to notice how solid he is. He smells masculine and woody, like he always does, but somehow it feels wildly out of place in a place that serves pancakes 24/7. My body wants to linger in it, and I have to consciously force myself to keep moving.

Behind me, Echo pauses and his attention shifts from me to the restaurant surrounding us. His gaze moves slowly, taking everything in. The emergency exits. The staff. The handful of early-morning regulars eating their meals. When he finally moves forward, it's with the same unhurried confidence he always has, and I fall in line beside him.

We slide into a booth near the window, and he has me take the seat facing away from the door. He sits across from me, folding himself into the tiny booth. His knees are angled awkwardly, his shoulders are crowding the vinyl, and his dark designer suit looks completely at odds with the mint-green seats.

He picks up a laminated menu curling at the edges, and I fight back a smile.

"What?" He asks.

"You look ridiculous."

He cocks a brow. "Okay, Bedhead Bambi."

My hands fly to my hair. Now he's the one fighting a smile.

"Relax. I was just joking."

"You joke?"

"Occasionally," he says. "I'm very selective about my audience."

I snort before I can stop myself. "Lucky me."

The corner of his mouth tips up and I feel myself smiling back.

A waitress appears at our table, holding a notepad in her hand. She's a pretty woman, probably a few years younger than me, with a high ponytail, winged eyeliner, and a bright smile.

"Morning," she says brightly. "What can I get you two?"

Echo looks to me.

"Coffee, please and can I also order the blueberry pancakes, but with no syrup?"

The waitress nods, scribbles it down, then looks at Echo. "And for you?"

"I'll do the same as her, but with syrup."

When she leaves, Echo tilts his head at me. "No syrup?"

"I don't like the fake stuff." I say. "Too sweet."

"Noted."

I narrow my eyes. "You don't need to file away facts about me like that."

"I absolutely do," he says calmly. "What kind of future husband would I be if I didn't?"

I shake my head, but I'm smiling again. Against my will.

The coffee arrives first. I add cream and sugar to mine, while Echo keeps his black. The food comes out a few minutes later.

Our plates hit the table, and I instantly deflate. Both stacks of pancakes are drenched in syrup.

It's not a big deal. It's not like it'll kill me, and I can try to scrape most of it off. I pick up my fork, already preparing to deal with it quietly.

"Excuse me, miss." Echo says, calling out to our waitress and stopping her short. "Hers was supposed to have no syrup."

"Oh, shoot. Sorry about that." She says, giving me an apologetic smile. "Let me get that fixed for you right away."

"Thank you." Echo says.

She takes the plate and disappears back toward the kitchen. I stare at the empty space in front of me.

"You didn't have to do that," I say.

"Yes, I did," he replies.

"I could've dealt with it," I add.

"I know," he says, taking a sip of his coffee. "But I'm here and you shouldn't have to."

A few minutes later my plate comes back perfect. No syrup and extra blueberries. I eat them slowly, letting the normalcy of the moment sink in. I'm eating pancakes with a killer.

A killer.

That's the word I keep using for Echo. The one I default to when I don't know what else to call him. It's neat, contained, and it lets me keep distance between us, even while we're sitting across from each other. Except it doesn't really fit him anymore. And it hasn't for a while.

Killers don't show up when you need them. They don't remember everything about you. Or prioritize your safety. Or treat you better than any other man ever has.

I take another sip of my coffee and watch him over the rim of my mug.

He's focused on his food now, smashing through the pancakes and smiling to himself.

I realize, distantly, that I haven't felt on edge the entire time we've been here. I didn't track who came in or out. I didn't clock the exits. I didn't brace myself for anything. I just existed.

Echo may be a lot of things. Dangerous. Sexy. Complicated. Capable of things I don't fully understand. But he's also the guy who was there for me when shit got really rough. And maybe… maybe it's time I stop calling him a killer long enough to see what else he might be to me.

I take another bite of my pancakes, still warm, still perfect.

Across from me, Echo glances up. "Good?"

I nod. "Yeah."

And this time, I actually mean it.

# CHAPTER TWENTY-SEVEN

SHE'S LOOKING AT ME DIFFERENTLY.

I noticed it at the diner, somewhere between her second cup of coffee and her last bite of food. It's subtle, a shift I'm sure most people wouldn't notice. But I'm not most people, and I notice everything. Especially when it comes to her.

Bambi's eyes are softer now, clearer. The hesitation I grew accustomed to seeing behind them is nearly gone, and the perpetual line of frustration between her brows has actually softened.

Even now, without even looking directly at her in my passenger seat, I can feel the difference in her gaze. Before last night, she couldn't look away from me fast enough. Now, her gaze lingers. She started staring at the diner and hasn't stopped since.

"Bambi."

"Yes?" She says, sitting up straighter in her seat.

"Stop staring at me. It's distracting."

She blinks and her mouth falls open.

"I am *not* staring at you."

"Yes, you are." I say smoothly. "You have been for a while. I would've said something sooner, but you know how much I like having your eyes on me."

Her cheeks turn a deep crimson and she grimaces as she crosses her arms over her chest. "I'm not staring, you egomaniac. I was just zoning out and thinking."

"About me?" I ask, giving her a sidelong glance as I tap my thumbs against the steering wheel.

"Actually," she says, narrowing her eyes at me, "I was thinking about how twisted the universe is. I mean, why else would it give such a pretty face to someone as narcissistic as you? It has to be some kind of cruel cosmic joke."

I glance at her and smile. "It's even prettier when you're sitting on it."

Her eyes flare, and the sound that comes out of her mouth is a mix between a laugh and a choke.

"What is wrong with you?" She manages. "You can't just say things like that."

"Why not?"

"Because it should be kept private."

"It's just us in here, Bambi."

"Still, there are rules—"

"Not ones I agreed to."

She turns in her seat to glare at me, trying hard to look angry and failing miserably at it. "You are deranged."

"And yet, you still want me around."

"When did I say that?"

"You invited me to breakfast."

"A momentary slip of judgement."

Her words sink in, and for some reason they hit harder than I expected. For a second, I sit there, unsure of what to say. I know we're giving each other shit, that this is what we always do to each other, but I can't help but wonder if that's what she really thinks.

"Is that what last night was, too?" I ask. Trying not to sound as invested in her answer as I am. "A mistake?"

"No." She says quickly, uncrossing her arms as her voice takes on a much softer tone. "I'm glad you were there."

I clench my jaw and stare out at the road ahead to keep my expression from doing anything I'll regret. "I am too."

The silence that follows is filled with words neither of us are willing to say out loud.

Our exit approaches in the distance, and I quietly shift into the right lane. I'm supposed to be taking her back to her bookstore. Back to her normal routine, and to the walls she's so carefully built around herself. Back to the version of her that won't let anyone see what she showed me today.

I clench my jaw and squeeze the steering wheel until my knuckles lose their color.

*I'm not ready to go back yet.*

*I might not ever be.*

I press my foot against the accelerator, and the exit that leads us back to Better Than Fiction comes and goes. Bambi catches it immediately.

"You missed the exit."

"I know."

She turns her head towards me and arches an eyebrow. "Are you going to take the next one?"

"No."

"Echo, what the fuck." She says, twisting in her seat and scowling at me. "What about my car?"

"I'm sure it'll be fine for a few more hours."

"And the store?" She asks, glancing down at the time on her phone before looking back up at me. "I'm supposed to open in an hour."

"When's the last time you took a day off?"

She opens her mouth and pauses, trying and failing to come up with an answer.

"Exactly."

She exhales through her nose and sinks back into her seat as her arms cross over her chest. The fire in her eyes dims slightly. "At least tell me where we're going."

I consider telling her before I think better of it and keep my mouth shut. There's no way to explain where we're going without explaining why, and there's no way to explain why without scaring her off.

"You'll see."

"I don't like surprises."

"I know." I glance over at her. "But you'll like this one." I pause. "You trust me?"

She's quiet for a beat, then sighs as she turns to look out her window. "Unfortunately."

***

THE SECOND WE PULL UP TO THE GATES IN FRONT OF THE Sannikov estate, Bambi's eyes go wide. She leans forward in her seat, and her lips part as she stares at the long driveway ahead of us.

I head up the driveway, and as soon as the house comes into view, she sucks in a breath.

"Is this where you live?" She asks, swiveling her head between both sides of the property.

I give her a nod.

"It's…" she pauses, chewing on her lower lip, "big."

I laugh. "It's not just mine. I share it with my brother and sister and our best friend." I cut the engine, slip out of the car, and open the passenger door.

"Come in with me." I say, nodding my head towards the house. "It'll be quick."

Bambi agrees, and she follows me inside, her footsteps soft on the marble floors. I can sense her taking everything in. The high ceilings, the expensive art on the walls. The luxury touches that don't announce themselves, but can't be hidden either.

I've lived within these walls my entire life. I know every room, every corridor, every corner. But seeing her in it makes it finally feel like home.

"Wait here," I say, guiding her into my room. "I'm just going to grab a key from my office. I'll be right back."

She nods, looking around the room like she's trying to piece together who I am based on my belongings.

I leave the room and head down the hall to slip into my office. The key is at the bottom of my desk drawer, and after digging for it, I pocket it and turn to leave.

"Hey." River says, standing in the doorway with his arms crossed and his expression unreadable. "You got a minute?"

"What's up?"

He glances down the hall towards my bedroom, where Dahlia is waiting. "You brought someone home."

"I did."

"You've never done that before."

"There's a first time for everything."

River eyes bore into mine, trying to read what I'm not saying. "Who is she?" He asks.

"No one."

The lie tastes wrong the second it leaves my mouth, and from the look on River's face, he knows it too.

"No one," he repeats slowly, stepping further into my office. "You don't bring 'no one' into our home, Echo. You don't miss work for 'no one.' And you sure as hell don't look like you've been put through hell for 'no one'."

I clench my jaw and glare at him, refusing to give him anything.

He studies me and I can see him trying to piece it together. "I'm worried about you," he says finally, sounding as exhausted as I feel.

That catches me off guard, and for a second I don't know what to say. River can be overbearing, and he doesn't always understand the way my mind works, but he's never been worried about me. Not like this, at least. "Why?"

"You've been different for weeks now. Distracted. Making mistakes." He shifts his weight. "Briggs told me about the interrogation. Said you weren't focused. Said someone almost got away because you were in your head."

My jaw tightens. "We handled it."

"Barely." He moves towards me, but there's no threat in his advance, just concern. "That's not you, Echo. You don't make mistakes. You don't lose focus. You don't bring people here." He pauses. "So, really, what's going on? What is she to you?"

*Everything.*

Nothing I can explain.

"I'm handling it," I say instead.

"That's not an answer."

"It's the one you're getting."

River exhales slowly. "You didn't check in last night. Athena was worried sick. She thought something happened to you."

Fuck. I should've called. I usually do when I know I'm not coming home, just so they don't assume the worst.

"She told me you haven't been sleeping," River continues. "That you've been disappearing at all hours. That you treat your phone like it's a lifeline." He pauses, and his voice drops. "This girl, whoever she is, she's got you twisted up in a way I've never seen before."

"I said I'm handling it."

"Are you?" He crosses his arms. "Because from where I'm standing, it looks like you're barely holding it together. And that scares the shit out of me."

I clench my jaw and swallow.

"Look," River says, his voice softening slightly. "If you care about her—"

"I do." The words are out before I can stop them. "I care about her more than I should. More than is smart. More than —" I cut myself off, running a hand through my hair. "Fuck."

River goes quiet, and when I look up, there's understanding in his eyes.

"How bad is it?" He asks quietly.

"Bad enough that I can't think straight when she's around. Bad enough that I haven't slept in weeks because I'm too busy making sure she's safe. Bad enough that—" I stop, because the rest of that sentence is too much, even for him. Bad enough that I'd blow my whole life up if it meant keeping her alive.

"Echo—"

"I know what you're going to say," I cut him off. "That it's a liability. That caring about someone makes you weak. That I need to get my head straight before it gets us all killed."

"That's not what I was going to say."

I look up, doing a shit job of hiding the surprise on my face.

River frowns at me. "I was going to say, be careful. Because someone who can make you lose focus like this? That's someone who can destroy you if you're not careful."

"I know," I say quietly.

"Does she know?" River asks. "How you feel?"

"No."

"Why not?"

"Because she's not ready to hear it. Because she's scared of this. Of me. And if I tell her, she'll run. So I'm giving her time. Letting her come to it on her own terms."

"And if she doesn't?"

I don't reply because I don't know what to say to that. Bambi and I are inevitable. I feel it in my bones, and I can't see this playing out any other way.

River watches me for another moment, then nods slowly. "Alright. But if whatever this is puts you or our family at risk, you need to tell me."

"It won't."

"You can't promise that."

"Yes, I can. I'll make sure of it."

For a second River looks like he wants to argue, but then he thinks better of it and steps aside to let me through.

"For what it's worth." He says, stopping me just as I brush past him. "If this is you happy, then I'm happy. We all are. I just hope she's worth it."

*She is.* I think to myself. *She's worth everything.*

# CHAPTER TWENTY-EIGHT

DAHLIA

I FIGURED ECHO HAD MONEY.

The car he drives gave it away. It's sleek, expensive, and rare. Something you can only buy when you have more than enough to spare. His clothes were also a tell. He never wears flashy designer logos or those god awful all-over-print patterns, but you can tell that everything he wears is expensive. Even without touching it, the quality of the fabric stands out.

But this? This is insane. I stand in the middle of his room, trying to wrap my head around it.

The house is massive. A sprawling estate with security gates, cameras at every angle, and grounds that look like they belong in a magazine. His room alone is bigger than my entire apartment, Fallon's room included.

He never gave off the impression of someone who lived in a mansion. He's too understated. Too controlled. And he never flashed his money around me. But the marble floors, the floor-to-ceiling windows, and furniture that probably costs more than most people make in a year. All of that tells a different story.

Echo isn't just comfortable. He's wealthy. Old money, maybe. Or new money so well-established it might as well be old. Either way, it's a reminder that I don't really know him. Not as much as I thought I did.

I move slowly through his room, taking everything in. The walls are painted a deep charcoal gray, almost black in the low light. A king-sized bed dominates the center of the room, covered in dark sheets and a thick comforter that looks ridiculously soft. There's a leather chair in the corner, worn at the arms as if he actually sits in it, and a bookshelf lined with titles I can't quite make out from here.

Oh, and the smell. It's him. That stupidly addictive, clean, woody scent clings to everything. The bedding, the air, the space itself.

I walk toward the dresser and let my fingers trail along the edge. He's always the one asking questions. Always the one learning about me, but here, I finally get to learn more about him.

On the dresser, there's a framed photo. I gently pick it up and stare at it. It's a picture of three boys and a younger girl. They're standing in front of this house, or at least it looks like it, with their arms slung over each other's shoulders. The girl is laughing at one of the boys. The other boy next to him is smirking. And Echo. Echo almost looks… *happy.*

It's so different from the version of him I'm used to that it takes me a second to recognize him. That must be his family.

I set the photo down and move toward the window. The view overlooks their perfectly manicured backyard and their Olympic-sized pool that looks like it's never been used.

I walk back towards the bed and press my fingers into the plushness of the comforter.

*Who are you, Echo? And why did you bring me here?*

I'm just about to take a seat on his bed when I hear voices. Faint but animated. Coming from somewhere down the hall. They're not yelling, but they're not quiet either. There's an unmistakable edge to both of their voices.

I move toward the door and press my ear closer, straining to hear.

"You brought someone home."

The voice isn't familiar. It's male, deep, and authoritative in a way that puts me a little on edge.

"I did." Echo replies, and even through the door I can hear the defensiveness in his tone.

"You've never done that before."

I should stop listening. I should give them privacy. I should focus on literally anything else. Instead, I find myself inching the door open a hair.

"There's a first time for everything." Echo says.

"Who is she?"

There's a pause, then.

"No one."

Echo's answer lands like a punch to the gut, but it shouldn't. I shouldn't be anything to him. In fact, everything I've been doing up until this point was designed to make sure I stayed just that. *So why the hell does hearing him say that sting so much?*

Before I can fully process my thoughts, the other man speaks again.

"You don't bring 'no one' into our home, Echo. You don't miss work for 'no one.' And you sure as hell don't look like you've been put through hell for 'no one'."

I press closer to the crack in the door, my heart hammering.

"I'm worried about you." The man continues. "You've

been different for weeks now. Distracted. Making mistakes. Briggs told me about the interrogation. Said you weren't focused. Said the guy almost got away because you were in your head."

My stomach drops because he's talking about me, about how I'm affecting Echo, about how I'm making him mess up at work, making him lose focus on things that are probably life-or-death in whatever world he operates in.

"That's not you, Echo. You don't make mistakes. You don't lose focus." He pauses. "This girl, she's got you twisted up in a way I've never seen before."

"I'm handling it." Echo says, but his voice sounds strained.

"Are you? Because from where I'm standing, it looks like you're barely holding it together. And that scares the shit out of me."

Another pause. Then.

"Look, if you care about her-"

"I do." Echo's voice cuts through, sharp and certain. "I care about her more than I should. More than is smart. More than-" He stops, and I can hear the frustration in the pause. "Fuck."

This is exactly what I was afraid of. Exactly what I've been running from since the night we met, and hearing it spoken out loud makes it real in a way I can't ignore.

"How bad is it?" The other man asks quietly.

"Bad enough that I can't think straight when she's around. Bad enough that I haven't slept in weeks because I'm too busy making sure she's safe. Bad enough that-"

He doesn't finish, but I can hear what he's not saying, can feel it in the weight of the silence that follows.

"Someone who can make you lose focus like this?" The

other man says, his voice taking on more gentle tone. "That's someone who can destroy you if you're not careful."

**Destroy.**

The word echoes in my head, bouncing around my skull until it's all I can hear.

I'm destroying him.

Christian couldn't think straight around me either. He lost focus in school. Made mistake after mistake until he made his final one. All because of me.

And now, without even realizing it, I'm doing it again to Echo. I'm making him lose sleep. Making him distracted. Making him unable to do his job properly. Making him vulnerable in ways that will probably get him killed in whatever dangerous world he lives in.

This is exactly what I swore wouldn't happen.

I promised myself after Christian that I would never let myself care about someone like that again, would never let my feelings turn someone into something dangerous and broken and self-destructive. But here I am, doing it anyway, letting Echo twist himself into knots over me while I pretend like I don't see what's happening, like I don't notice the way he's unraveling.

"Does she know?" The other man asks. "How you feel?"

"No."

"Why not?"

"Because she's not ready to hear it. She's scared of this, of me, and if I tell her, she'll run." He pauses. "So I'm giving her time. Letting her come to it on her own terms."

My throat tightens because he's right. If I had any idea he could feel this way about me, I would've ran. I would've never admitted I was attracted to him and I definitely wouldn't have had sex with him.

"If whatever this is puts you or our family at risk, you need to tell me."

He's talking to his brother.

He has to be.

"It won't." Echo replies.

"You can't promise that."

"Yes, I can. I'll make sure of it."

More silence, and then his brother speaks up again. "For what it's worth, if this is you happy, then I'm happy. We all are. I just hope she's worth it."

I step back from the door, not wanting to hear his reply because I already know the answer.

I'm not worth it. I'm not worth the trouble, or the risk, or the fucking danger. I'm just not.

I sink down onto the edge of his bed, feeling numb and completely out of body.

*I can't do this to him.*

Echo steps into the room and I force myself to look up, even though every instinct is screaming at me to run.

He stops when he sees me, his eyes scanning my face like he's trying to read something there. I wonder if he can see it. The guilt, the fear, the knowledge that I'm destroying him just by existing in his space.

"You okay?" He asks.

I nod even though it's a lie. "Fine. Just tired."

He doesn't look convinced as he watches me with those intense green eyes that see too much.

"Come on." He says, reaching his hand out for mine. "Let's get out of here."

I stand without argument because what else am I supposed to do? Tell him I overheard? Tell him I know I'm destroying him and I need to leave before it gets worse? Tell him that everyone I care about ends up broken and I can't watch it happen again?

*No.*

I follow him out of the room, down the hall, and back to the car, and I don't say a word, like the fucking coward I am.

I can tell myself that the timing is wrong, or that I'm still processing, but the truth is, I don't say anything, because I don't want to. And that, above everything else, is the most selfish thing I've ever done.

# CHAPTER TWENTY-NINE

DAHLIA

THE CITY DISAPPEARS BEHIND US, SWALLOWED BY TREES AND winding roads that narrow with every mile.

I watch the landscape change through my window. Buildings give way to forest. Paved roads turn to gravel. The signs, what few there were, start to vanish.

We're off the beaten path now. Way off.

I shift in my seat, hyper-aware of how isolated we're becoming. There are no streetlights. No other cars. No people at all. Trees press in from both sides, and the windy road we're on feels like it's leading to nowhere.

Echo pulls up to a gate and hops out of the car to unlock it. As I watch him, I shift uncomfortably in my seat.

*What am I doing?*

No, seriously, what the fuck am I doing?

Not running away as soon as I realized how he felt about me was bad enough, but letting him take me somewhere private, knowing full well that my rational brain stops functioning every time we're alone, is completely unhinged.

Echo slips back into the car and glances at me. "Almost there."

I nod and give him a tight smile.

He drives up a long dirt road, and as we round a bend, the trees open up, revealing a lake that's so pristine and so blue it doesn't even look real. There's a wooden dock stretching out over the water, weathered and slightly uneven, and beyond it, nothing but lush trees and open sky as far as I can see.

Echo parks his car off to the side and cuts the engine.

I stare through the windshield, taking it all in. The water. The trees reflected on its surface. The complete and utter absence of anyone else.

"What is this place?" I ask quietly.

"Come see for yourself."

Echo steps out of the car and leads us to a wooden bench near the shore. He takes a seat, and for a second, I stand there awkwardly behind him, not knowing what to do.

I know we've just spent the last few hours in close proximity, but after everything that's happened, something about the contrast between the limited space on the bench and the open scenery around us makes sitting next to him feel way more intimate.

I'm about to stick to standing when I notice Echo shift. He's trying to be subtle about it, but at 6'6, I don't think anything he does goes without notice.

Echo slides to the very edge of the bench, so much so, that I'm pretty sure the edge of it is digging into his right ass cheek.

I shake my head.

Only Echo would risk a splinter in his ass just to make me feel less awkward about sitting next to him.

I hate how well he works around me. How he adjusts. He

has this innate ability to anticipate my needs before I can even recognize them, let alone verbalize them.

He gets me, but he shouldn't.

I take a seat on the other edge of the bench, close my eyes, and listen. To the rustling of leaves. To the soft lapping of water against the shore. To my own breathing, finally slowing.

"What are we supposed to be doing here?" I ask, opening my eyes to look at him.

Echo glances at me. "This."

I frown. "Sitting in silence?"

He nods.

"Why?"

"You said that was your favorite way to spend a day off."

*He remembered that?* Of course he did. He remembers everything. Every throwaway comment. Every minor detail I've shared without thinking. He catalogs everything about me like some kind of fanatical Dahlia Delacruz historian.

"Yeah," I say quietly, sinking my teeth into my lower lip to stop from smiling. "It is."

We fall into a comfortable silence again. I keep my eyes on the water, but in my periphery, I'm hyperaware of everything about him. The way his shoulders rise and fall with each breath. The way his fingers tap against his knees. The way his gaze keeps drifting toward me when he thinks I'm not paying attention. I catch him looking more than once, but I pretend not to notice.

"Thank you." I say quietly, my eyes catching his. "For being there for me last night. It wasn't your problem to worry about, but you showed up anyway."

"Your problems are my problems, Bambi." He says quietly.

I glance at him, and his expression is as unreadable as ever, but when I look into his eyes, I can tell he means it. And that absolutely guts me.

Standing here by this beautiful lake, hearing him say things like that, it's easy to forget what I overheard. Easy to pretend that this is harmless. But nothing about this feels harmless anymore.

"Well, either way." I say, fidgeting with my hands in my lap. "Thanks."

He nods and stares out at the lake again. I do the same, but my mind stays focused on him.

We sit there a while longer, saying nothing as the sun drifts lower and lower, until the sky starts to bleed with streaks of purple and gold. Shadows stretch across the water, and a cool breeze moves through the trees. I rub my hands over my arms, more out of instinct than anything, and beside me, Echo shifts.

"We should probably head back," he says quietly.

I nod, glancing once more at the water before pushing to my feet. "Yeah," I murmur. "Probably."

We rise from the bench at the same time and accidentally head towards each other. For a moment, we stand there. Closer than we were on the bench, and even closer than we were in the car.

Echo reaches up to tuck a strand of hair out of my face, and when his fingers graze my neck, he lets them linger.

"Your pulse is racing again, Bambi." He says, locking his eyes on mine.

He tilts my chin up and I swallow, knowing exactly where this is going.

Before today, I would've let this happen. I would've let Echo do whatever he wanted to me, and I would've convinced myself that I had it under control. But now I know none of this is under control, and that's exactly why I have to stop it, even if it hurts.

I take a step back, averting my gaze as his hand falls to his side. My body mourns the loss of his touch immediately, and it takes everything in me not to lean back into him.

He looks at me, searching my gaze. "What's wrong?"

*Nothing. This feels too easy. Too good. Too much like the one thing I can't let myself fall into and nothing like the friendship I've been trying to force us into.*

*Friends.* That label doesn't fit us anymore, and as I look up at him and feel that undeniable pull, I'm not even sure it ever did.

*But maybe it needs to.*

If I can shove us back into that box, I might still be able to control this. I can stop this now before it gets any worse.

"Sorry," I say, clearing my throat. "Still friends, right?"

I watch the way the word lands and see him process it. "Yeah," he breathes, giving me a nod with his jaw tight. "Of course."

I look back at the lake because I can't bring myself to look at him anymore, and when Echo finally heads back to the car, I trail a few feet behind him.

We drive back into the city in silence, and when we finally pull up to the bookstore, Echo still doesn't say anything as he opens my door for me.

I get out of his car and head towards my own, parked a few spaces down. Echo watches me get in, and as always, he doesn't pull away until I'm already on the road.

I watch him in my rearview, and when he finally takes a turn and disappears, the strangest wave of grief slams into me.

I'm losing him. Not entirely. He's still in my life and he'll probably text me before I even make it home.

But what we used to be... that messy, undefined, terrifying yet thrilling thing with no name and no rules, is over now. And I can't even be sad about it, because I'm the one that killed it.

# CHAPTER THIRTY

*Echo*

She called me her friend.

I crack my neck and tap my fingers on the steering wheel to try to distract myself from the thought, but it digs in deeper.

*She called me her fucking friend.*

Bambi has hidden behind that label since the moment we met, and it never once bothered me. Partly because I knew it was just a guise meant to cover up the truth of what was really happening between us. And partly because every time she said it, I could tell she didn't mean it.

But this time it felt different. Final. And the way she pulled away from me? That shit was the most painful thing I've ever experienced, and I've been beaten to the point of passing out more times than I can count.

It's like that word ripped a fucking hole in my chest, and now I'm just sitting here hemorrhaging all over the place.

I pull the car to a stop at a red light and grit my teeth hard, hoping the pain will distract me from my pathetic thoughts. When that doesn't work, I escalate.

*Friend.*

I punch the steering wheel with full force.

*Friend.*

I punch it again, harder this time, and the ache in my knuckles is a sweet distraction. I punch it again, and again, and again. Watching as the flesh over my knuckles rips and my steering wheel gets splattered with the evidence of madness.

A horn blares from somewhere behind me, but I don't stop. I couldn't even if I wanted to. I need this release, like I need fucking air.

Friend. Friend. Fucking. Friend.

I press my forehead against the wheel and grip the sides of it, breathing through my nose as I try to remind myself of who the hell I am. Of what I am.

Someone bangs on my window, and I glance over to find a middle-aged white man standing outside my door.

He's red-faced and balding, wearing a stained t-shirt that stretches just a little too tightly over his midsection. He's screaming at me through the glass.

I reach for my gun, not even bothering to be discreet about it, and aim it at his shiny bald head.

The fucking prick stops yelling and his red face turns white at an impressive speed. He raises his hands with wide eyes and nearly trips over himself as he backs away from my car.

*Goddamnit*, I'm slipping. I know I am. I just threatened an inconsequential asshole because a girl called me her friend and I couldn't handle it.

That's where I'm at right now.

That's what Bambi has reduced me to.

I press the back of my bleeding hand against my mouth and stare at the road ahead.

*When the fuck did this happen?*

My phone lights up on the passenger seat, and I glance at it. Three missed calls from River. Two from Briggs. And a string of missed texts I can't read from here, but the most recent one from River is visible in the preview.

Come home. Now. It's urgent.

I look at my hand, at the gashes in my knuckles, and the blood dripping down to my wrist. Then I clench my jaw, take my foot off the brake, and drive like it never even happened.

---

I STEP INTO THE DARK LIVING ROOM AND MY EYES immediately spot the two silhouettes waiting for me. River is leaning against the wall with his arms crossed and his jaw locked tight. Briggs is seated on the couch beside him, watching me with a wary expression.

"What's going on?" I ask, eyeing the two of them.

River's eyes drop to my hands for a beat, noticing the cuts there, then he wordlessly reaches for the remote.

The flat-screen flickers to life, and a video plays of what looks to be dash cam footage. It's grainy and dark, but the timestamp in the corner of the screen is unmistakable.

August 15th.

The night I met Bambi.

*Fuck.*

My throat tightens, but I school my features and keep my mask of indifference firmly in place.

The footage continues to play, and at first, there's nothing there. Just shadows and the faint glow of a streetlight bleeding into the frame.

Then she appears.

Bambi backs into the frame, moving cautiously, as if every step back towards the wall costs her something.

My jaw clenches.

Four figures emerge in front of her. Their faces are indistinguishable, but I know it's the men I killed. I'd recognize their builds anywhere.

The biggest one goes after her first, backing her against the side of the building. He lunges for her, but just before he reaches her, she ducks. The movement is so fast I almost miss it. One second she's cornered, the next she's dropping low, out of view.

When she comes back up, there's a knife in her hand. She swings it wildly, all desperation and adrenaline, and the blade catches the side of his face. Even through the grainy footage, I can see the spray of blood and the way he staggers back as his hands fly to his face.

The others freeze for half a second, shock rippling through them, then they attack. All of them. All at once.

The second man grabs for her. She twists out of his grip and slams her shoulder into his chest. He stumbles back, but it doesn't seem to do much damage. The third one comes at her next. She swings the knife again, and he jerks back just in time, leaving the blade to slice through empty air.

"She fucking stabbed him!" He shouts, his voice crackling through the speakers, and I couldn't be prouder.

*Yeah, she fucking did.* Bambi's a fighter through and through.

The fourth man reaches for his waistband. For the gun tucked there. And my pulse spikes.

She sees it too. I watch her body tense, watch the split-second decision flash across her face. Then she runs at him. Straight at the man with the gun.

*Jesus Christ. This is what was happening while I was unconscious.*

She slashes wildly, going for anything she can reach. Messy. Uncoordinated. Completely chaotic.

He curses and slams his elbow into her back. She goes down hard and it takes everything I have not to look away.

The second her body hits the pavement, all four of them close in. Rough hands grabbing. Ripping. Yanking at her dress, her hair, anything they can reach.

Those motherfuckers. I'd give everything to raise them from the dead, just so I could kill them again, slower this time.

Someone pries the knife from her hand, and I watch with my jaw clenched as she gets dragged back to her feet. One of the bastards puts her in a chokehold.

She kicks. She claws. She fights like hell. But he's stronger, and now he's lifting her off the pavement.

Her movements start to slow. Get weaker. But she still isn't done fighting. She tries to headbutt him, but she misses. And to get back at her, the coward slams her face into the brick wall.

The sound echoes through the speakers. Wet. Sickening.

My hands are shaking. I curl them into fists to make it stop, but it doesn't work. I've already lived this moment. I was there. I felt the rage boiling under my skin. The split-second decision to intervene. The satisfaction of putting them down one by one. But watching it now is different. *Worse.*

Because I'm standing here helpless, watching her get hurt all over again. I force myself to stay still. To keep my face blank. River is watching me. I can feel it.

On screen, the gunshots start and the men drop one by one. Bodies hitting the pavement in sequence like dominoes. The camera doesn't catch me, but it catches her. Standing there. Frozen. Staring at the bodies. Then, looking up and staring at me.

A jacket is tossed at her. *My jacket.* Then she runs off screen and the footage cuts to black. Silence fills the room.

River turns to face me. His expression, unreadable in the worst possible way. "That footage was taken from a parked car in that alley way," he says. His voice is calm. Too calm.

I drag my hand through my hair and rub the back of my neck.

"You told me there was nothing to worry about."

"There isn't." I hiss. "She's not going to say anything."

"How could you possibly know that?"

I hold his gaze and River's eyes narrow.

"You know her, don't you?"

I stay quiet.

"Jesus Christ, Echo. Is she the girl you brought here? The one you've been seeing?"

"I'm not seeing her." I say, feeling annoyed at the implication. "We're just friends."

Briggs snorts from across the room.

I ignore him.

River doesn't. "Since when have you made a habit of befriending liabilities?"

"Since now."

His jaw tightens. "Do you know where I got this footage?"

I shrug. Even though my pulse is hammering. Even though I already know the answer is going to be bad.

"The police are circulating it." River says. "Along with every other criminal organization in the city, not to mention every independent contractor on his payroll. He's offering two hundred thousand dollars to anyone with information leading to her whereabouts. He wants her found, Echo. Do you get what I'm saying?"

I swallow.

*Yeah. I understand.*

"She's in danger," River says. "We all are."

I already knew that. I've known it since the second I let her walk away that night. Since I started tracking her phone and monitoring her location and posting guards outside her bookstore like some obsessive fuck who can't let go. But hearing River say it out loud makes it real.

"She needs to come stay with us," River says. "It's the only way we can be sure Casello won't get his hands on her."

"What if she doesn't want to?" I ask.

I realize how stupid the question sounds the second it leaves my mouth. *Since when did I give a fuck about what anyone else wanted?*

River's expression hardens. "She doesn't have a choice."

He's right. I know he is. She doesn't have a choice, and neither do I.

I look at the screen one more time. At the freeze-frame of Bambi running away. Her eyes wide with terror. Helpless. Exposed. Exactly the position I never wanted her to be in again. And here she is, anyway. Because of me.

"We need to go get her now." I say. "Before someone else does."

River nods. "I'll come with you. Let me just pull the car up front."

I nod, even though I hate everything about this.

River heads for the door and I push off the couch to follow him, but Briggs stops me short. "You sure about this?"

"About what?"

"Bringing her here. Into this." He gestures vaguely at the house. At the life we've built. The empire. The violence. The shit we do that normal people don't come back from. "You know what that means, right? Once she's in, she's in. There's no going back."

"I know."

He studies me for a moment. "Yeah, but does she?"

It doesn't matter if Bambi knows what she's getting into. She's in danger, and her safety supersedes everything else. Including her freewill.

I'll make sure Bambi leaves that apartment tonight. Even if I have to drag her out of it, kicking and screaming.

# CHAPTER THIRTY-ONE

DAHLIA

THE SCENT OF SMOKE DRAGS ME FROM SLEEP. NOT THE screaming fire alarm. Not the heat licking across my skin. Smoke. Thick, wrong, invasive, and filling my lungs like wet cement.

I bolt upright and gasp.

*Bad fucking idea.*

My lungs reject the action, and I cough violently. Each breath, broken glass and razor blades that shred through my chest and scrape my throat raw.

I force my eyes open, trying to see through the haze. Smoke is everywhere. Rolling across the ceiling in thick gray spirals. Seeping down the walls like lava.

*What is this?*

I swing my legs over the bed and my feet hit the floor. The hardwood is warm. Wrong. Everything is wrong.

"Fallon!" I try to shout, but my voice comes out strangled. Raw. Like someone took a sander to my throat. I stumble toward my bedroom door and yank it open.

The hallway is an inferno. Flames devour the far wall

near the kitchen. Orange and alive and so fucking hungry. They crawl toward me like they recognize me, like they've been waiting for me to show my face. My body freezes as my mind slips to a different fire on a different night.

*This can't be happening.*

*Not again.*

Heat slams into me like a physical shove, pulling me out of my memory. I stagger back and jerk my arm up, shielding my eyes from the embers and ash floating in the air.

The smoke is so thick I can barely see two feet ahead of me. My eyes burn. My throat burns. Every breath feels like I'm inhaling glass.

"Fallon!" I scream, louder this time.

A door slams open down the hall, and she stumbles out, coughing. Her eyes are wide and terrified when they lock on mine.

"What's happening?" She chokes out.

"Fire. We need to get out. Now.

She nods and we move together toward the front door as flames spread across our bedroom doors like they're racing to trap us.

We reach the front door and I grab the handle without thinking.

Pain explodes across my palm.

"Fuck!" I hiss, yanking my hand and cradling it against my chest.

The metal is scorching. Blistering. The skin of my palm, already hot and angry.

"There's fire on the other side," Fallon says, grabbing my other arm and pulling me away from the door. "We need to find another way out."

She's right.

I look around, desperate, but Fallon's already two steps ahead of me.

"The patio." She says, jerking her head toward the living room.

*Right.*

As we stumble toward the sliding glass door, my lungs scream for air, but there isn't any to be found. Just heat and smoke and the crackling sound of everything we own turning to ash.

Fallon reaches the door first and tries to pry it open. "It's stuck." She gasps, giving me a panicked look.

I step beside her, and we both pull. Still, the door doesn't budge.

Melted, probably. Or warped from the heat.

"Move!" Fallon yells, grabbing a chair. I jerk out of the way, and she hurls it at the window with full force.

The glass shatters outward in a violent spray, and cool air rushes in. Beautiful and clean, everything my lungs are screaming for.

We both rush onto the patio, gasping. For half a second, relief floods through me.

*We made it. We're out.*

Then, the fire inside roars to life.

The fresh oxygen feeds the flames, and they surge forward with renewed hunger. Heat intensifies so fast it singes the hair on my arms and burns through my clothes.

Fire crawls up the wall. Spreads across the side of the building like something alive. Something hunting.

"Fuck!" Fallon scurries back, slamming into me.

I pull her away from the doorway, and we both keep moving until our backs hit the patio railing.

Trapped.

Again.

"What do we do?" Fallon asks, her voice cracking between coughs.

I look over the edge. Four stories down. Too high. Way too fucking high. The fall would kill us faster than the flames would.

"I don't know."

*We're trapped.*

The realization settles over me and weighs me down like a physical thing.

Fallon grabs my hand and squeezes so hard it hurts. "I love you." She says, her eyes shimmering with unshed tears.

*I love you too.* I want to say it back. I want to tell her she's everything to me. That she saved me from myself when I thought I had nothing left to live for. But the words are lodged in my throat.

I squeeze her hand back. Harder. Hoping she understands. Hoping she knows.

Fallon smiles as her eyes slowly drift closed. I close mine too, bracing for the end. For the heat. For the smoke to finally win.

Then I hear a crash. A loud and violent one coming from somewhere inside the apartment.

My eyes snap open.

"What-"

Another crash. The front door explodes inward, sending splinters of wood flying in every direction. Through the smoke and flames, shadows move.

*No.* Not just shadows. Men. Two of them. Tall. Broad-shouldered, and cutting through the inferno like it's nothing. Acting as if the flames don't singe their clothes and the heat doesn't scorch their skin.

I see Echo first, and relief swells inside of me. His name tears from my throat before I can stop it.

*He's here.*

*How is he here?*

*How did he know?*

My brain fires questions faster than I can process them. Between the pounding in my head and the ash coating my lungs, nothing makes sense.

"Bambi!" He shouts, his voice rough and desperate as his eyes cut across the living room. "Where the fuck are you?"

"Here!" I scream back, and I'm crying now. Tears streaming through the soot on my face. "Over here!"

His head whips toward the sound. Our eyes lock. And then he's moving. Fast. Purposeful. As if nothing in this world could stop him from reaching me.

He reaches us on the patio, and the second he does, his arms wrap around me.

"I've got you." He says, his voice rough and strained in a way I've never heard before. "I've got you."

I try to speak. To ask what he's doing here. To ask how he knew. To tell him I'm not going anywhere without Fallon. But before I can, the other man appears through the smoke.

He looks like Echo. Same height, same build, same dark hair, but where Echo is all sharp edges and danger, this man is... different. Softer features. Warmer eyes and skin. But the way he moves? Just as lethal. He must be his brother.

He doesn't say anything when he sees me staring at him. He just gives me a quick nod before scooping Fallon up and throwing her over his shoulder.

Then they're both moving.

Echo leads the way, navigating through the smoke and flames in my apartment like he's walked this floor plan a thousand times. Like he's memorized every obstacle. Every exit.

I think about asking him how he's doing that, but decide

against it. Partly because it doesn't matter right now and partly because I don't want to know.

I bury my face in his neck, trying to block out everything. The ash. The flames. The way him being here makes me feel a strange warmth in my chest that has nothing to do with the fire.

His skin smells like smoke and sweat and that signature woody scent that's distinctly him.

I grip onto him tighter as he takes the stairs down two at a time. Each step jolts me, making my pounding headache worse, but I don't care. We're almost out. Almost safe. Almost—

Cold air hits my face the second we make it outside. Clean. Fresh. Beautiful. I gasp, pulling it greedily into my lungs, and coughing hard.

*We're out.*

*We made it.*

Relief hits so hard, my whole body goes limp.

I try to lift my head. Try to look at him. Try to say thank you, or I'm sorry, or something that matters. But the edges of my vision are already going dark, and it feels like I'm slipping underwater.

Echo's saying something. His mouth is moving. But I can't hear him over the ringing in my ears. I can't focus on anything except the way his arms tighten around me. Like he's afraid to let go. Like he thinks I might disappear if he does.

Then… nothing. Just darkness. And the distant wail of sirens fading away.

# CHAPTER THIRTY-TWO

## FLASHBACK

DAHLIA

*Age 16, Franklin Springs, Georgia*

*I CRACK MY BEDROOM DOOR OPEN AND MY STOMACH GROWLS AS the mouthwatering scent of Dad's Chicken Adobo wafts down the hallway. I didn't even have to ask him to make it tonight. He just knew.*

*I stand in front of the mirror and adjust the gold locket necklace they got me, admiring how pretty it looks as it catches the light.*

*"Happy Birthday, Anak." Mom said, fastening it around my neck. "I can't believe my baby is already 16."*

*I smile to myself.*

*It really is super pretty.*

*My parents wanted to throw a big family party tonight to celebrate the occasion, but I insisted on keeping things simple.*

*I'm sixteen, practically an adult, and if they threw the kind of party they wanted to, they would've absolutely rented a jumpy house for my little cousins, which would've been totally mortifying.*

*A quiet dinner with just the three of us is more than perfect.*

*Tap. Tap. Tap.*

*The knock on my window startles me and I turn to find my boyfriend Christian standing there grinning with his hand pressed against the glass.*

*I rush to him and open the window.*

*"Happy birthday, Dollface." He says, flashing me a broad smile.*

*I look at him and my heart does that stupid little flutter thing it always does whenever he's around.*

*"What are you doing here?" I whisper, my eyes bright. "My parents are right down the hall. They'll kill us if they find you out here."*

*Irritation briefly flickers across Christian's face before his magnetic smile slides back into place. "It's your day, beautiful. There's no way in hell I was going to let them stop me from seeing you. Besides, I've got a birthday surprise for you. Come on."*

*My parents don't exactly approve of me dating Christian. They were open at first, but when my grades started slipping and they found out I was spending almost everyday with him, they insisted I cut it off. I didn't, of course. I just started seeing him behind their backs and figured with time, they'd eventually learn to accept him.*

*"I don't know." I hesitate, worrying my lip. "We're about to have dinner and dad made my favorite. I can't just—"*

*"Please Dollface," he says, cutting me off. "I swear it'll only take a minute."*

*I glance back at my open bedroom door. Mom will be calling me to come eat any minute now. But Christian looks so excited. And he drove all the way over here. The least I could do is go see his gift.*

*"Okay." I say, climbing out of my single story window. "But only for a minute."*

*His smile widens. "That's all I need."*

*I've snuck out this way dozens of times, but as I follow him away from the house, a sinking feeling settles over me.*

*"Why don't you just bring it over here?" I ask, stopping a few feet away from my window.*

*Christian's smile falters.*

*"I just, want to be able to hear, if they call for me."*

*"Come on, Doll." He says, grabbing my wrist. "Trust me. You're going to love it. "*

*He leads me down the lengthy driveway and when we reach the road, he releases his grip and turns to face me.*

*"Dahlia Nocon," he says, his face contorted into a pained smile. "I love you so much it hurts. These last six months have meant everything to me, and I honestly can't imagine spending another day without you by my side."*

*"I can't either, baby." I whisper, smiling up at him.*

*Christian sighs and smiles back at me. "I was hoping you'd say that. Now, I know this may seem crazy, but..." He pauses, reaching into his pocket to produce a tiny blue velvet box and lowering himself to one knee. "Will you marry me?"*

*I stare at the thin solitaire diamond ring nestled inside in utter disbelief.*

*No.*

*What was he thinking?*

*I love him, but I'm not ready for that. Neither of us is.*

*Christian searches my face, and the weight of his stare suddenly feels suffocating. He's waiting for an answer, and I still haven't said anything.*

*"It's beautiful, but—"*

*"But what?" He asks, cocking his head. His smile doesn't waver, but there's a shift in his gaze.*

*"We can't," I manage to choke out. "I... I can't."*

*His smile falters, and he stands up to his full height.*

*"Why not?" He asks, his tone sharp and demanding. His hand reaches out to touch me, and I instinctively pull it back.*

*The air between us crackles with tension.*

*"My family..." I stammer, grasping for any excuse that might stop whatever this is from escalating. "My parents would never allow it."*

*"You don't need to worry about that." He says, and something about the confidence in his words makes my brow furrow.*

*"I can't just not worry about it, Christian. They're my parents. I'm not getting married without their blessing."*

*"Trust me, Dollface." He murmurs, closing the distance to gently cradle my face. "You won't need it. Now please, make me the happiest man in the world and say yes."*

*I wrinkle my nose and glare at him, trying to decipher his words. "What do you mean? Why won't I need it?" I ask, searching his face for answers.*

*"Because it's already been taken care of." He whispers, his mouth curving into a wide smile. "I took care of everything, doll. Now answer my question."*

*Dread twists in my stomach. "What are you talking about?"*

*His jaw ticks and he presses his lips into a thin line.*

*"Christian, what are you talking about?" I ask again, my heart slamming in my chest.*

*He sighs and slowly shakes his head. "See for yourself."*

*He nods his head towards the house, and I whip around and nearly collapse at the sight in front of me.*

*My house is on fire.*

*I try to rush forward, desperate to get to my parents who must still be trapped somewhere inside, but Christian is faster. His arms wrap around me and pull me against his chest in a suffocating grip.*

*"Let me go!" I scream, fighting against him. "Let me go!"*

*I try to fight him off. I try to kick and claw with every ounce of strength I have, but it's futile.*

*He's too strong and I'm too goddamn weak.*

*"It's pointless." He hisses, his voice chillingly calm as he presses his lips to my ear. "I slit their throats before I even lit the match."*

*My legs give out underneath me and if Christian wasn't holding me, I'd collapse.*

*They're dead. My parents are dead.*

*Christian killed them before he came to my window.*

*Before he fucking smiled at me.*

*Before he proposed.*

*He killed them and then came to claim me, like some kind of prize.*

*A guttural scream tears from my throat, raw and threaded with pain, so much pain.*

*"Shh. It's okay." Christian says, trying to console me. "You don't need them anymore. You have me."*

*I try to stop screaming, but the sound only intensifies as I stare at the bright orange flames engulfing my home. It's as if what's happening is too much for my brain to process, so my body's natural impulses are taking over.*

*Christian curses under his breath and clamps his hand over my mouth, but my screams still persist.*

*"Stop." He hisses, tightening his grip. "Why are you acting like this? Don't you understand? This was the only*

*way. They would have never let us be together. They were always going to keep you away from me."*

*Scalding tears stream down my face as he holds me there and forces me to watch the flames grow higher. Hotter. Consuming everything I love. Everything that made me feel safe.*

*"I love you, Dollface." Christian croons, pressing his lips to the top of my head. "And I always fucking will."*

# CHAPTER THIRTY-THREE

DAHLIA



White walls, white ceiling, white light. For one disorienting second, I think I'm dead. That my soul is floating in some sort of ethereal void that exists somewhere between this life and the next.

Then, I notice the details that don't make sense. The crown molding in the corners of the walls. The steady beep of medical equipment somewhere nearby. And the ornate light fixture in the center of the room that probably costs more than my car.

I don't think I'm dead. But if what happened last night really happened, I might as well be.

"She's awake." Fallon whispers, scooting her chair closer to the side of my bed. She leans forward and her blonde head pops into view.

"Who—" I start, wincing at the sting in my throat. "Who are you talking to?"

Fal's expression shifts, and for a second I wonder if

maybe I am still dreaming. Everything feels a little delayed, like the world around me is still buffering.

Fallon's eyes cut to something on the other side of the room, and a small smile tugs at her lips. "Your boy's been here all night." She whispers softly. "Hasn't moved from that chair once."

My heart does that stupid stuttering thing I hate, and I turn my head slowly, following her gaze to the left side of the room. Echo is sitting in a leather armchair by the window, his body completely still except for the steady rise and fall of his chest. His clothes are destroyed, covered in soot and singed in a few places, and his hands are wrapped in thick bandages that are stained with blood.

He looks like he's been through hell, but it's his eyes that gut me. They're red-rimmed and hollow, locked on mine with a crazy intensity that steals whatever breath I have left.

"Hi." I say weakly, giving him a half-smile.

He doesn't smile back. He just stares at me and clenches his jaw.

*Is he… still mad at me?*

Fallon stands up and smooths her hands down her soot-covered jeans. "I'll go and let the doctor know you're awake."

She's out the door before I can stop her, and then it's just us.

I look at Echo. He looks at me. And neither of us says anything as silence blankets the room.

Echo shifts, and when his back brushes against the back of the seat, he lets out an involuntary hiss.

"You okay?" I ask, studying his face.

He nods, but I notice him lean forward so that his back doesn't touch it again.

*He must be hurt there, too.*

I take a moment to assess my own damage. I don't have a single mark on me. Not one burn. Not one blister. Not even a bruise. Echo shielded me from everything.

Just like he has been since the day we met. Just like he did with those men in the alley, and with Josh at the grocery store and restaurant. Echo has been trying to protect me, in his own messed-up way, and I hate that he had to burn in order for me to see that.

"How are you feeling?" He asks, his voice rough.

"Alive." I say, feeling tears brim in my eyes. "Thanks to you."

Something shifts in his expression, but before I can really process it, it's gone.

"Don't thank me, Bambi." He says, picking at a loose thread on the seam of the armchair. "I don't deserve your gratitude."

My brows pull together. "Why would you think that?"

Before he can answer, the door swings open and Fallon and Echo's brother enter the room with a man in his early sixties. He's holding a tablet and even without a lab coat on, I can tell he's a doctor by the way he's carefully assessing me.

He introduces himself, checks my vitals, and runs through a list of things I should watch for over the next few days. I nod when it seems appropriate, but honestly, I'm not really listening. I'm watching Echo, who's still watching me.

On the other side of the room, Echo's brother says something quietly to Fallon. She replies without looking at him, and he says something else that must piss her off, because she presses her lips together and looks at the ceiling.

The doctor wraps up, excuses himself, and leaves.

I'm still looking at Echo and he's still looking at me, but neither of us are saying anything.

"D." Fallon says, stepping up to the side of my bed. "We should talk." She glances at Echo's brother. "Can you two give us a minute?"

He gives her a nod and heads for the door. Echo exhales through his nose, then pushes off his chair and quietly follows him out. As soon as the door closes, Fallon turns to me.

"So, the damage to the apartment is pretty extensive. And River and I were talking."

"River?"

"Echo's brother." She says quickly, weirdly averting her gaze. "Anyway, we were talking, and he thinks it's best if we stay here for a while, and I agree."

"At the hospital?"

Her brows pull together, and she shakes her head. "This isn't a hospital, babe. We're at their estate. This is just their medical room. After the medics cleared you, Echo insisted on bringing you back here so his own doctor could check on you."

"Oh…" I say, still trying to wrap my head around everything. "So wait. You want to stay here? With them."

"Well, want is a strong word. And I've had more time to sit with it than you have. But yeah, until we figure out who started that fire, it makes the most sense."

A cold feeling slithers down my back. "How do we know someone did? Couldn't it have just been faulty wiring or a bad outlet?"

"The fire marshal is investigating it. Because of the damage, it'll be a few weeks before they have anything definitive."

"But they think it was intentional?"

She exhales. "Our unit was the only one that burned. And with Christian out there, I just don't want to take any chances."

*Christian.*

I hadn't even let my brain go there yet. I'd been so focused on Echo that I hadn't even stopped to think about who might have actually started the fire. But now that Fallon says his name out loud, I can't stop thinking about it.

"You think this was him?"

"I don't know." She says, honestly. "Maybe. Or maybe it was just bad wiring and we're worrying over nothing. Either way, I'd rather err on the side of caution in a gated mansion than at some shitty motel we can barely afford."

Christian burned my life down once. I wouldn't put it past him to break out of prison just to do it again.

"Okay." I say, tilting my chin up.

"Okay?"

"Yeah." I say, pulling the thin blanket tighter across my lap. "We'll stay here for now. At least until they figure out how the fire started."

She reaches out to squeeze my hand. "I'll go find River and let him know you agreed."

She slips out, and for the first time since I woke up, I get time alone to process.

Christian is out there somewhere, and after what just happened, there's a good chance he's found me. Echo saved my life tonight, but then said he didn't deserve my gratitude. What the hell did he even mean by that? And why was he looking at me so strangely?

The door opens again, and Echo quietly steps in. He heads for the chair by the window and sits down, careful not to let his back touch the seat this time.

"Did you have the doctor look at it?" I ask, fidgeting with my hands under the blanket. "Your back, I mean."

"He doesn't need to." He says quietly. "I'm fine."

I swallow. "Echo, I don't think you are."

"I said I'm fine, Dahlia."

I give him a nod and try not to be bothered by the fact that he didn't call me Bambi.

The room goes quiet again, amplifying every single sound in the distance. I can hear the wind outside, moving through the trees, and somewhere in the distance I hear laughing. I think it's Fallon's, which is odd, but it's so far away that I can't be sure.

I stare at Echo's hands. At the thick layers of bandages wrapped around his palms and fingers. At the way his fingers twitch, like they hurt even now, when he's sitting perfectly still.

He's in pain. Because of *me.* No wonder he's acting so distant.

I had spent months convincing myself Echo was bad for me. That getting closer to him will only end in disaster. I built an entire case against him and reminded myself of it every single time he got too close.

But as I stare at the second-degree burns on his skin and the prominent dark circles under his eyes, I realize with startling clarity...

Echo isn't the dangerous one.

*I am.*

And now, less than twenty-four hours after I tried to shove us back into the friend zone, I'm moving in with him.

This is going to be a fucking disaster.

***To be continued...***

*Dying to know what happens next?*

*Make sure to grab the next book in
the Lovesick Sinners series:*

**You Were There For Me**

283

***Want more from Jessa?***
*Signup for my free newsletter
At www.jessahalliwell.com to receive exclusive access*

# FEAR

# JESSA HALLIWELL

# FEAR THE REAPERS
# CHAPTER ONE

## STEVIE

My body jolted at the sound of a hushed whisper filling my ear.

"Stevie."

Disoriented from sleep, I rubbed my eyes and waited for the hazy figure standing next to me to come into focus. Recognition clicked and relief seeped into me. It was just Alex.

*Fuck*. It was *Alex*.

"Shit. What time is it?" I asked, swiping the drool from the corner of my mouth and almost spilling the bowl of cereal I had fallen asleep next to.

"It's 4:37. I waited for you, but got worried when you didn't show. I got a ride over here." She said with a grimace.

"Fuck. We have to go. Now." I said, shooting up from the kitchen table as I stuffed my feet back into my beat-up white sneakers.

Sleep evaded me again last night, making a quick power nap at the kitchen table turn into almost six hours of sleep.

"I'm sorry." Alex grimaced, pacing back and forth, "I didn't know what to do. I mean, I couldn't just leave you here alone."

Her heart was in the right place, but she knew better than to come home alone. Especially during one of Malcolm's benders. Malcolm had a routine. We may not count on him as a parent, but my dear stepdad was always consistent. He was a barely functioning drug addict. He held a job, albeit a pretty shitty one. Every Friday, he'd get off of work at 4:00 PM on the dot, pick up his drugs, shoot up, and lock himself up in the house for the weekend.

Fridays, Saturdays, and Sundays were the days we made ourselves as scarce as possible. We had a system, and I had just royally fucked it up by falling asleep. Naps during the day seemed to be the only thing that worked for the nightmares, but I should've known better. I just prayed we both wouldn't have to pay for my stupid mistake.

Slinging my bag over my shoulder, I grabbed Alex's hand and pulled her towards the front door. Passing through the hallway as quietly as possible, every step we took made my stomach drop a notch further.

Maybe he wasn't home yet. Maybe if he was, he wouldn't notice us. Maybe he'd already smoked and would be too high out of his mind to pay us any mind. Maybe.

We were a few feet from the door, when out of nowhere, the door flung open and in walked Malcolm.

"Where the fuck do you think you're going?" He spat, catching us mid escape.

Still in his uniform of a navy blue jumpsuit, he spread out his arms and acted as a blockade between us and the door. Leaning forward, he inched his face towards mine and the bitter stench of sweat and stale cologne hit my nose.

Anytime Malcolm would shoot up, he would douse himself in cheap cologne, trying to mask the foul scent only desperation and days of not showering could give him. The fresh wounds and dilated pupils on his gaunt face were also dead giveaways that he was already high as a fucking kite. *Fuck.*

"We were just leaving." I mumbled, pushing Alex behind me.

"No. You know the fucking drill. Hand over the cash." He ordered with a smug smirk.

"What? No!" Alex asserted as her eyes darted between the two of us. "I saw her leave you an envelope full of cash two nights ago. We pay you rent once a month."

"She hasn't told you." He said with a smirk as his dull eyes flashed towards mine.

"Told me what?" She hissed, keeping her eyes trained on the man she refused to acknowledge as her father.

"She pays when I tell her to. Period. If she doesn't, she knows exactly what the fuck will happen." He didn't need to say anything further for Alex to understand the threat in his tone.

I fixed my gaze on the floor as shame licked across my skin. Everything Malcolm said was true. I wanted to tell Alex. To talk about the abuse I encountered daily at the hands of her father. But how could I reveal such an awful secret without destroying the trust between us?

"You are an asshole!" She screamed, trying to claw her way towards Malcolm's face. "God, what the fuck was Carla thinking having a child with a lowlife like you!"

The mention of our mother's name wiped the smirk off of Malcolm's face. His lip twitched, and he cocked his head to the side. I knew the warning signs of Malcolm's violence like the back of my hand. I could see what was coming and with only seconds to act, I shoved Alex as fast as I could and jumped into her place in time to receive the full force of his punishing blow.

His fist collided with my cheekbone and the impact of his swing sent my body careening for the ground. The room went quiet as my back hit the hard linoleum floor with a crack and both of their eyes followed my descent. I watched the contents of my bag spill out and scatter across the floor, and my heart sunk to the pit of my stomach. Laid out for all of us to see was the forty dollars I had set aside for groceries that week.

I glanced at Malcolm and could see the hunger in his eyes. Money fed his addiction, and he didn't care who he harmed to get his fix. Without hesitation, he reached down, grabbed for the cash, and tucked it into his pocket as if it had always belonged to him.

I wanted to kill him. To kick and scream and claw for my money back. But fighting him was pointless. He would only get more aggressive if I tried to stop him and with Alex here, I couldn't risk it. I could deal with his violence, but she shouldn't have to.

Malcolm disappeared before we even had time to process what happened. That was the one redeeming quality about my stepfather. Once he got what he wanted, he left us the hell alone. At least until the next time he needed something.

"Why didn't you tell me?" Alex whispered as she helped me pick up the contents of my bag.

My words lodged in my throat. What was I supposed to say? I lied because it was easier. I lied because I didn't think she could handle the truth and it was the only way I could protect her. I lied because it was what I always did.

Alex was still in her last week of high school and whether she liked it or not, my job as her big sister was to keep her safe. I was the one who could afford the bruise already forming on my cheek. She couldn't. Her teachers would ask questions, and CPS might try to take her away. Alex was Malcolm's biological daughter. Because of our mother's passing, he had full custody of her until she was eighteen.

We tried to run away before, but once Malcolm realized

that the money disappeared, he reported her missing. The cops found my car and shit hit the fan. Alex almost had to repeat ninth grade, and I barely escaped criminal charges.

In two weeks, she'd be eighteen and we could be free of Malcolm and this fucking town for good. But until then, we needed to keep a low profile and avoid him as much as possible. June 16th couldn't come soon enough.

# FEAR THE REAPERS
# CHAPTER TWO

## TRISTAN

"To what do we owe the pleasure?" Atlas asked, leaning into the blue crushed velvet seat.

His dark eyes meticulously grazed the man standing before us as his thumb mindlessly twirled the ring on his middle finger. It was mental manipulation at its finest and At was doing a hell of a job of fucking with the man.

To the untrained eye, his casual posture came off relaxed, bored even. But simmering below the surface was an insurmountable amount of pressure. I could see it in the slight tick of his jaw and the tension radiating off his shoulders. He sat poised and ready to strike at the idiot requesting our audience.

"I… I have something to offer the four of you," the dick mumbled, "as payment for my debt."

"Interesting." Cyrus noted, his eyes trained on the twitching junkie that stood before us. "We don't know you. You don't know us. So how is it you owe *us* something?"

How he emphasized the word "us" had the man nearly shitting himself. At this point they were toying with him, like children playing with their food. Everyone in this town knew that if you so much as spoke ill of The Reapers, you were as good as dead. This motherfucker had to have a death wish for showing up at our club unannounced.

"I, uh… know Johnny. Your dealer on the west side of town? I've come into a little debt with him and he… uh…

one time when he was high off his ass, he told me where I could find you."

Johnny was a dead man for two reasons. One, he sent this asshole to Hell's Tavern to find us, and two, he sampled the product. Our club was our sanctuary, and we hired our employees under one condition; they stayed clean. Johnny fucked up, and by the murderous look in Ezra's eyes, Johnnyboy's hours were dwindling.

"And the canary finally sings." Atlas mocked, standing up from his seat. The man eyed his every move and I could almost taste the fear that oozed out of him. Atlas' hands moved to smooth the wrinkles in his jacket before reaching into his pocket and pulling out his phone.

"Ez," he said, grabbing my older brother's attention, "he's all yours. The rest of us need to make a few *arrangements*."

By arrangements, he meant tracking down Johnny's ass. Drug distribution was just one of the many businesses our syndicate ran, and to put it bluntly, keeping track of a dealer was beneath our pay grade. But Johnny made himself our problem. If he was talking freely to this asshole, who knows who else he was talking to. We needed to send a message and nothing compared to the personalized ones we hand-delivered.

At the mention of his name, Ezra leaped to his feet and stalked towards his new prey, cracking his neck as a smile brimming with malice spread across his face.

"Ple... Please! Wait!" The man cried, waving his arms around frantically. "It's an excellent offer, take it and I'll leave town and never say a word of this to anyone."

His pleas fell on deaf ears as Ezra's movements didn't falter. Ezra enjoyed the hunt almost as much as he enjoyed the kill, and this man looked like he'd be stupid enough to put up a fight. Poor fuck had no clue fighting back would only intensify Ez's torture.

"I… man… please." The man pleaded, his blown-out eyes frantically darting between the four of us.

Maybe it was the smell of desperation that wafted towards us the moment he entered the club. Maybe it was just my morbid curiosity. But I wanted to see what he offered.

Cuing them all in on my thoughts, I cleared my throat and nodded towards the man. I wasn't one for words, especially around strangers, but my brothers understood. The subtle message was all they needed to figure out where my head was at. It was the dynamic we'd always had, even before the stutter.

The one thing you can rely on in life is family. It was the reason we kept our leadership small, with each of the four of us heading different aspects of the business. We had a chain of command for whatever remedial tasks we needed, but we only truly trusted each other. That small circle of trust was the key to sustaining our power over Caspian Hills for the last six years.

"It's not every day that a meth-head comes looking for us." Ezra hissed as he approached the man cowering beneath him. "This offer of yours better be worth your life. I was looking forward to watching your pathetic body bleed out."

The man's face inadvertently ticked when the word "meth-head" tumbled into his ears. The term clearly bothered him and I smirked to myself at the irony. He was high off his ass, not giving a fuck about jeopardizing his own life by being here, but still cared about what complete strangers thought of him. The fragility in his eyes was almost humanizing. Almost.

The world is full of sinners, some are just better at keeping their sins hidden from view. While men like

Malcolm were desperate to conceal their flaws, my brothers and I took on a more unapologetic approach.

We were brutal business men and when the time called for it, lethal killers. Did we deny it? Of course not. We embraced our demons, bathed in the blood we spilled, and lived up to our fucking reputation. That's how my brothers and I earned the name The Reapers. People knew that when we came for you, death was calling and your time was up.

Caspian Hills was ours, and no one was stupid enough to fuck with what was ours. The men who tried didn't live long enough to gloat about it.

The man standing before us had willingly walked into a lion's den. He was either incredibly brave or remarkably stupid. Based on the interaction so far, I was betting on the latter, with or without the meth that was probably coursing through his system.

"I have someone for you. A girl." The man stammered, smiling eagerly.

I had no clue why this man thought offering a girl to us would change his fate. In our world, women were a dime a dozen. People either wanted to be us or they wanted to fuck us. We emanated power and even if they didn't know who we were or what we did for a living, they could sense that shit from a mile away.

"We don't deal in flesh." Atlas glowered, giving the man a look of utter disgust. The sheer force of his words wiped the man's stupid smirk off his face.

"She's worth it." He pleaded, his body trembling. "Blonde bombshell. She'll do anything you tell her. She'll earn her keep. Th..th-think of her as an investment that keeps on giving. I ran it by Johnny and he wanted her for himself, but I knew you were the ones with the actual power here."

*Fuck.* We now had a dilemma on our hands. If we didn't

take what he offered, Johnny would run his stupid mouth, if he hadn't already, and word would spread across town that The Reapers had gone soft. We didn't want that kind of publicity. Not when The Diaz Cartel was hungry for ammo to use against us. Tired of slumming it in Caspian Valley, they were looking for any cracks in our foundation.

We could kill the bastard here and now. I could practically see Ez's demon begging for the bloodshed, but then we'd have a bigger mess to clean up and frankly, the asshole wasn't worth the hassle.

Taking the girl would send a message and help cement the fact that we always collected our debts. She'd stay with us until we grew bored with her and as long as she did nothing stupid to get herself killed, we'd let her go once the dust settled. We'd solidify our reputation and our men wouldn't have another body to bury. No harm, no foul. Looking towards my brothers, I could see that they were all slowly drawing the same conclusion.

"Okay, asshole." Atlas boomed, tossing a business card on to the coffee table. "Send the girl to this address at midnight tonight and disappear. If we see your face again, we will kill you. If you try to escape without fulfilling your end of the deal, we will kill you. Understand?"

The man nodded his head rapidly as he grabbed the card, stuffed it into his pocket, and scrambled for the exit.

"Not so fast." Cyrus ordered, halting the man's jerky movements.

"Ez, he's all yours." Atlas mumbled without sparing the man another glance.

"Wha- wait, I thought we had a deal?" The man cried, getting hysterical.

"Oh, we do and you better deliver." Cyrus interjected, tilting his head slightly. "You didn't honestly think you could come here uninvited and leave unharmed, did you? I know you're a meth-head, but you can't be that fucking stupid."

The man's eyes grew wide as terror raked through his entire body. Ez relished in his fear, flashing a wicked smile as he stalked towards the man. We all stood up and moved to get a closer look.

The unmistakable smell of piss filled the room as the trembling man backed himself up against a wall. *I felt for whoever had to clean that shit up.*

Blow after blow, Ezra pounded into the man's clammy flesh until his own scarred knuckles bursted from the force. The man's brow had split open and I could see the bruises already forming on his sickly pale skin. The man's legs had given out on him and he crumpled to the floor in a heap of bones and bloodied flesh as he desperately tried to block Ez's savage blows.

"Let this be a reminder, you piece of shit." Ezra spat, wiping the sticky mixture of blood and sweat from his brow. "Never fuck with The Reapers."

He gave him one last punishing kick to the gut before walking away with a little skip. Ezra looked elated as he made his way back towards us. It would've seemed shocking to those that didn't know him, but there was nothing Ezra enjoyed more than pure, unfiltered violence.

"Hell," Ezra quipped, looking at the blood splatter all over his black oxfords, "that's my third ruined pair this month."

"Maybe you need to switch up your finishing move?" Cyrus joked, nudging me with his elbow.

"Nah, you boys love a good splash show." Ez said with a wink. "I can't disappoint the fans."

"You're a s... sick fuck." I mused, shaking my head.

Ez blew us a kiss as he headed back to the lounge, making

me and Cyrus chuckle. The fucker was the craziest one out of all of us, and that was really saying something.

"Alright, dickheads." Atlas spoke up, garnering all of our attention, "That's enough action for the evening. Let's get back to business, shall we?"

As security dragged the man's unconscious body away, we all retook our seats in the back of our low lit VIP area as if nothing happened.

It was just after 5:00 PM and the club didn't open for another few hours. That gave us plenty of time to get the floors cleaned and have the guards prepare our house for our newest asset.

Poor thing had no clue that her piece of shit pimp had just sold her freedom. No idea that her mind, body, and soul no longer belonged to her.

If we were better men, we'd let her go. Unfortunately for her, my brothers and I were never raised to be good men.

# FEAR THE REAPERS
# CHAPTER THREE

## STEVIE

I COULD FEEL ALEX'S EYES ON ME AS I WIPED DOWN THE tables for the fifth time in a row. I'd been avoiding her for most of my shift, but I could only dodge her attention for so long. It was getting close to closing time, and I'd already finished most of the pre-closing duties. Soon we'd be driving back home, and I'd have to face the questions brimming behind her eyes.

Even though Alex was six years younger than me, in a lot of ways, she and I were equals. We had gone through the same hardships together and were both thrown into adulthood sooner than we expected. The one major difference between me and her was I didn't allow myself to feel anything while she, ironically, felt everything.

Alex was the epitome of an Empath and sometimes, my need to shield her from the cruelties of the world outweighed my instinct to treat her as an equal. I lied to my little sister about what went on when she wasn't around. Though my intentions were pure, it didn't stop her from feeling betrayed.

What she witnessed wasn't anything new. Malcolm always resorted to violence when he didn't get his way. But after years of hiding it from her, everything was hitting her all at once.

"Everything okay?" Alex asked, pulling me out of my thoughts.

I was so stuck in my head; I didn't even realize I was wiping down her table.

"Yeah, sorry." I said, taking a seat across from her, "Just a little tired. How's the homework going?"

"Good, I guess." She paused, tapping her pencil against her notebook. "You think you'll get out early tonight?"

Her emerald eyes glanced around the barren coffee shop.

"We close in ten minutes," I said, giving her a small smile as I pulled a cookie from my apron pocket, "hopefully no one else comes through."

I stuffed half of the cookie into my mouth, swallowing the lie I told right along with it. That night, there was someone I hoped to see. The same person who, for the past two years, was my last customer almost every night.

He and I met by chance nearly two years ago. One of the other baristas called out for her closing shift, forcing me to stay and work opening to closing. I could use the extra over-time, so I took it in stride. Little did I know what that night had in store.

It was a rainy Tuesday night in the middle of October, and Cafe Au Lait was vacant. Tapping my fingers against the reclaimed wood countertop, I sliced my eyes at the clock that refused to budge. The caffeine high of the morning rush disappeared, leaving me feeling jittery, yet exhausted. By 8:30 PM, I gave up waiting for customers and started the closing process. The streets were vacant, and I doubted anyone would come in that late.

Just as I began mopping the floors, in walked Mr. Tall, Dark, and Delectable at 8:59 PM on the dot. It took a special asshole to come into a place one minute before they closed without so much as an apologetic smile. His shiny and most likely designer shoes tracked in mud-soaked leaves from the sidewalk and I cursed underneath my breath, knowing I'd have to sweep again.

"8 ounce doppio cappuccino. Dry. Extra hot." He barked with his ear pressed to his cell phone. There was nothing that irritated me more than bad manners, and this guy was exhibiting all of them. He didn't even bother to look at me when he barked his order into the air.

"Name." I chirped back, out of sheer habit.

The moment my mind realized what I said, blood came rushing to my face. There was no one else in the cafe. Why did I ask for his stupid name?

"You need my name?" He asked, glaring at me as he broke off the call.

Fighting a smile, he looked around the empty cafe as if to make his point even more obvious. I know there's no one else here, asshole.

"I'll have it right out for you, sir." I responded sweetly, ignoring his question and attitude completely.

I had mastered the art of telling people what they wanted to hear, and this guy looked like the type to get a hard-on from people kissing the ground he walked on. His entire demeanor screamed power. The pristine suit, the wide stance, his perfectly quaffed dark hair, even the formal tone in which he spoke told me everything I needed to know. He and I were nothing alike.

I plastered on my fakest smile and turned towards the espresso machine, trying to bust out his stupid cappuccino as quickly as possible. Of course he had to pick one of the hardest drinks to make. God, he would be a 'dry cappuccino' kind of guy.

"Just for future reference, dickface," I hissed under the sound of the steaming milk, "we close at nine and just because you're sexy as fuck doesn't mean that you get to be an inconsiderate asshole."

"Dry Cap." I called out, sliding the cup forward on the handoff plane and not even bothering to look up. He wanted to be rude? Well, two could play that game.

For a split second, warm fingertips grazed mine. The alien feeling created this delicious sensation that blanketed my entire body. Warmth. Comfort. Safety. No man's touch had ever made me feel that way and for a few beats, I stood there dumbstruck, staring at my fingers like they were malfunctioning. Before I could process what happened, he slipped out of the shop and back into the dark night.

*What the hell was that?*

Shaking the thoughts of the stranger out of my mind, I went back to cleaning and cursed at myself for being so eager to leave to begin with. I should've waited until 9, like I was supposed to, and I would've avoided creating double the work for myself.

Thirty minutes later, I stepped out into the chilly autumn night and tugged my flannel across my chest. A grey t-shirt dress and light flannel was cute during the morning, but was practically masochistic at night. The wind's frigid bite sent Goosebumps spreading across my bare legs. I cursed as I grit my teeth. If I didn't die from freezing my ass off, I was going to kill Marie for calling out sick.

It was eerily quiet out and something in the air felt off. I couldn't pinpoint what it was, but my body felt the presence of danger. I spent a few seconds staring out into the darkness and looking for any signs of a threat, but all I saw were a bunch of vacant cars and empty streets. It wasn't exactly safe to be in downtown Caspian alone this late at night, and had I known I'd be closing, I would've gone for a closer parking spot.

Seeing no immediate signs of a threat, I turned around to lock the door behind me. The second I turned my back, a throat cleared and my body froze. On reflex, I whipped my body towards the sound and nearly fell over when I saw who it was.

"Hey." He said, barely containing the smile he was trying to fight.

"Jesus Christ! Dry Cap? You scared the hell out of me." I exclaimed, pressing my hand against my racing heart. "What the hell are you still doing here?"

"Sorry, I wanted to make sure you got to your car okay. It isn't safe in this part of town, and I couldn't leave you by yourself in good conscience. Since you closed at 9," he said, flashing me a knowing grin, "I figured I wouldn't have to wait long."

Had he heard me? I wanted to die. Like, have a higher power remove me and any traces of my big, stupid mouth from this earth. *Nice one, Stevie.*

"It's fine." He offered, seeing my discomfort. "I was an asshole. Hearing that my face resembled a cock was brutal, but I definitely earned the verbal lashing."

*It didn't.* At all. It was a stupid handsome face on what looked like a stupid perfect body. He had a sharp, chiseled jawline peppered with the perfect amount of scruff. Dark, full brows that framed his sultry brown eyes and thick lashes that most women would kill for. The most alluring part of his face was his mouth. He had the most perfect smile I'd ever seen, and his lips looked like they could make even the filthiest words sound beautiful.

Before I could think of a clever or witty comeback, he had already turned on his heel and began walking. And after a moment of shock, I quickly caught up with him.

"Which one's yours?" He asked, nodding his head to the row of cars lining the street.

"The uh... the Focus." I chirped, still in disbelief at how this night had turned out.

"You shouldn't park so far." He noted, keeping his eyes on the sidewalk ahead. "A girl like you could get in a lot of trouble this late at night."

A girl like me... I didn't know whether to be flattered or annoyed. DC had already made an assumption about me, and we'd known each other for all of thirty minutes. Then again, I made my own quick assumptions about him and he was already proving them wrong.

By the time we arrived at my car, I realized we walked the rest of the trek in silence.

"Well, we're here." He said, gesturing to my car.

I nodded and gave him a small smirk. I didn't know what to say. 'Thank you' seemed lame and 'see you later' seemed presumptuous. But he didn't miss a beat.

"See you around..." He paused, letting his eyes roam my breasts unabashedly. "Stevie."

My heart slammed in my chest as my body rebelled against the calm composure I tried to cling on to. The name tag, Stevie. He was only reading the name tag. *Get a hold of yourself and pussy, don't you dare quiver right now.*

In that moment, as his golden brown eyes roamed my body, I felt exposed and objectified and strangely excited. No one had ever looked at me like that, let alone caused my body to react so strongly to a damn look. The rush was addictive. I wanted more.

From that day forward, I requested to close on every shift I worked. It was stupid, but I secretly hoped we would meet again and I'd have more chances to feel that rush.

Two years later, our meetups had sort of become our

unspoken rule. Almost every closing shift Dry Cap or DC as I liked to call him, would show up, order his drink, and hang out to make sure I made it safely to my car.

For nearly a year, I refused other guys' advances. I waited for DC to make a move that never came. I could never be in an actual relationship. I learned the hard way that there are too many emotional expectations that I just couldn't deliver on. But sex was fun and uncomplicated, and well, my body wanted him. But every night, he'd walk to his car, I'd walk to mine, and we'd go back to our lives as if nothing happened. As if the spark crackling between us was a hoax.

Alex usually stayed at a friend's house while I worked, but after that close call earlier, I wanted to keep my eye on her. Maybe it was a good thing that he hadn't shown tonight. I hadn't spoken a word about him to Alex. I told myself it was because we'd be leaving eventually and it didn't matter anyway, but that was a lie.

The truth of the matter was, I cared about him. Probably more than I should've. When his piercing eyes looked at me, it was like he was looking deep within my soul, seeing each fucked up layer. But instead of being repulsed by what he saw, he embraced it.

I rarely laughed at his jokes, but it didn't seem to bother him. Other guys I'd dated in the past couldn't handle the blow to their ego, but DC didn't seem to care. He had this quiet confidence about him that made me feel at ease. I didn't have to worry about my reactions offending him. Carla's conditioning was still so deeply ingrained into me that my body still feared expressing emotions, even eight years after her death.

Overtime, I grew to be more comfortable with this formidable stranger than I was with my own flesh and blood. Alex was my sister, and I loved her to death, but we couldn't have been more different. She was warm and trusting, while I was cold and suspicious. She was tan, svelte, and cool blonde, while I was pale, curvy, and deep brunette. She was spunky and outgoing, while I was quiet and closed-off.

But in him I found a kindred spirit. I enjoyed pretending that in a different life, he and I could be something more. Something beyond this pseudo security guard/confidante relationship that we had fell into so easily.

I debated asking him for help with Malcolm once, when one of Malcolm's fits of rage resulted in a cracked rib, but I didn't want whatever the dynamic between us was to shift. He viewed me as a normal person, not some girl with a fucked up life. The last thing I wanted was for him to take pity on me. I couldn't stand seeing that look in his eyes.

Almost as if thinking of him had brought him into fruition, the sound of the fan over the door kicked on, showing that someone had walked through the door.

"Be done soon." I mouthed as Alex popped her headphones back in with a nod.

Butterflies swirled through my stomach the moment my eyes caught sight of his familiar 6'3 frame. As usual, DC came in dressed impeccably. He probably worked in law or finance because after two years, I had yet to see him without a sharp suit on.

Tonight was no different. He walked in the cafe wearing a perfectly tailored navy suit with a crisp white button-up shirt that made the healthy glow of his skin stand out.

"Hey DC, the usual?" I called out as I breezed by him.

I purposely kept things platonic with us after realizing that nothing more was coming from this. He didn't need to know that my stomach did flips every time he walked into the room. Or that my traitorous pussy pulsed every time his seductive scent of smoky sandalwood and soft amber surrounded me.

Without warning, his large hand encased my arm in a gentle, yet solid hold, halting my movements. I whipped my head to face him. He had never grabbed me before and it was so unlike the polished man I knew. The look on his face was cold, dangerous, and lethal.

"Who did it?" He hissed as his sharp jaw ticked and his large body trembled with what looked a lot like rage.

"What the hell are you talking about?" I asked, brows furrowed in confusion.

I had never seen this side of him before.

"The bruise that's blooming on your face, Stevie." He said, his fingers gently grazing the tender flesh. "Who did it?"

My hand involuntarily floated towards his. It had probably gotten worse over the last couple of hours. *Shit.* I had been in such a rush to get the hell out of there, I completely forgot to cover it up.

"It's nothing." I lied, faking a smile as I chewed the inside of my cheek. "I clumsily tripped right into a door knob this morning."

It disgusted me how easily the lie spilled from my lips. I never wanted to lie to DC, but he had backed me into a corner. Omitting was one thing, but this was a flat out lie and it made me feel awful. But his pity would have felt worse.

"You tripped." He deadpanned as his sharp brown eyes pierced right through me.

"Yes, so… the usual?"

I didn't wait for a response. Moving towards the espresso bar, I could feel his eyes probing and assessing me as I made his drink. The force of his gaze made me want to shrivel up into a little ball and confess all of my sins, but involving DC would only lead to more trouble. I was leaving in less than two weeks. I could keep our secrets until then, even if he ended up hating me for it. *He'll end up hating me anyway for leaving without saying goodbye.*

DC left the shop without saying another word to me. I hoped that he'd be outside waiting, but after I locked up the shop, there was no sign of him.

I told myself that it was better this way. I was only prolonging the inevitable. Maybe seeing the mark on my face gave him an insight into how messy and imperfect my life truly was. He had no room in his perfectly tailored life for the chaos that consumed mine.

Want to read more of Stevie's story?
Start the Lovesick Villains Series Today

Dear Reader,

Thank you for taking the time to read book one of Echo & Dahlia's story! If you had a good time, please consider leaving a review or sharing it on social media. It helps me so so much and I literally couldn't do what I do without your support.

I had such a good time writing Echo & Dahlia's story, and if you thought book one was crazy, book two is going to blow your mind. Expect a lot of twists and turns, and of course that insane chemistry that makes Echo & Dahlia's relationship so fun.

Thank you so so much for reading, and I can't wait to give you many more stories soon!

xo
Jessa

# ALSO BY JESSA

*Fear The Reapers*
*A Lovesick Villains Trilogy: Book 1*

*Queen of The Reapers*
*A Lovesick Villains Trilogy: Book 2*

*Wrath of The Reapers*
*A Lovesick Villains Trilogy: Book 3*

*Twisted Violet*
*A Lovesick Villains Standalone*

*I'll Be There For You*
*A Lovesick Sinners Duet: Book 1*

*You Were There For Me*
*A Lovesick Sinners Duet: Book 2*

# ABOUT THE AUTHOR

*Jessa Halliwell* is a Dark Romance Author who writes about angsty, torturous love mixed with a dash of danger and suspense. She loves writing romance only slightly more than she loves reading it. She's been known to binge read novels then spend the rest of the day sulking over the massive book hangover.

Jessa resides in Northern California with her fiancé and her sassy German Shepherd Mix named Nugget. When she isn't writing, you can find her obsessing over her skincare routine, drinking an unhealthy amount of hibiscus tea, or probably crying over a really good book.

Follow me on tiktok: @jessahalliwell
Follow me on IG: @jessahalliwellauthor
Join my Facebook Readers Groups: Jessa Halliwell's
Lovesick Villains